"Just what does Mr. Ford think about you investigating a strange man at this hour of the night?" Sam asked.

*What about Mrs. McPhee?* Mackenzie wanted to ask. "There is no Mr. Ford," she managed.

Sam's near smile turned his face into a series of strong lines and angles. "So why are you spying on me, Mack?"

Mackenzie quickly averted her gaze, not about to tell Sam the real reason she'd tracked him down. "Why not?" she returned coyly. Looking into Sam's eyes again, she couldn't believe he was really jobless and homeless, as he claimed to be. *Oh, no,* she thought. *Was she really falling for a vagrant?*

Dear Reader,

You're about to behold a "Rising Star!"
Four of them, to be exact. This month, we're
launching into the galaxy of American Romance a
new constellation—the stars of tomorrow...four
authors brand-new to our series.

And they're just in time to celebrate with us the tenth
anniversary of American Romance. In honor of this
occasion, we've got a slew of surprises in store this
year. "Rising Star" is just the beginning!

Join me, then, and welcome Laraine McDaniel, the
author of one Harlequin Intrigue novel, to American
Romance.

Laraine has been inventing stories since her
childhood. So, in adulthood, it was no surprise that
she found herself coming up with inventive
characters, such as her homeless hero Sam McPhee
in *One Foot in Heaven*. Laraine makes her home in
Arizona, with her husband and family.

Don't wait another minute. Turn the page and catch
a "Rising Star"!

Sincerely,

Debra Matteucci
**Senior Editor & Editorial Coordinator**
**Harlequin**
300 East 42nd St.
New York, NY 10017

# Laraine McDaniel
## ONE FOOT IN HEAVEN

# *Harlequin Books*

TORONTO • NEW YORK • LONDON
AMSTERDAM • PARIS • SYDNEY • HAMBURG
STOCKHOLM • ATHENS • TOKYO • MILAN
MADRID • WARSAW • BUDAPEST • AUCKLAND

This book is dedicated with love to
Mildred McDaniel,
Mother extraordinaire

Published August 1993

ISBN 0-373-16499-8

ONE FOOT IN HEAVEN

# Prologue

"What happened to you, Mr. McPhee?" the doorman asked, tipping his hat.

The apartment building was one of those high-priced D.C. affairs, at Fourteenth and L streets, and Sam McPhee liked living there only marginally more than he liked practicing law for the city.

"I got mad and quit my job today," Sam said, then noted the flash of surprise in the doorman's eyes.

"Bad day, sir?"

"Did your life ever flash before your eyes?" he asked the uniformed attendant.

Sam had felt something snap inside himself today, like a toothpick. Immediately he'd known things would never be the same.

"Boy, I envy you, Mr. McPhee," the doorman said. "Having the courage to risk taking a chance like that."

Sam grimaced. He'd saved his own skin today, but he knew braver things had happened in D.C.

The silver doors of the elevator stretched apart, and he strode toward them. Inside, he leaned back and massaged the back of his neck. Life in the nineties had its benefits, but the wonders of the twentieth century could also work against you. An automated teller had just informed him that he had no money. He sent up a silent prayer that his wife would have an explanation.

The mahogany box rose swiftly to the eighth floor. Moments later, Sam found the building's superintendent waiting for him outside his apartment.

"I'm sorry, Mr. McPhee," the super said, producing a ring of keys. "If it had been up to me, I wouldn't have changed the locks."

"What the hell?" Sam sucked in his breath, and the air whistled between his clenched teeth. "Where's Alva—? Where's my wife?" Something definitely wasn't right here. "I want answers, and I want them now."

"Here," the super said, pressing an envelope into Sam's hand. "Your wife left this for you."

All day Sam had thought about stretching out in a tub filled with water as hot as he could stand it. He'd envisioned lying back, his legs hanging over the side, a Cuban cigar in one hand, a bottle of beer in the other. Home.

With an uneasy queasiness in the pit of his stomach, Sam opened the envelope and found a letter wrapped around his Swiss army knife. A measure of relief washed through him. He'd have hated to lose that knife. Then one of his colleagues' names jumped off the page like a nasty insect, and the rest of the letter blurred. Something about a divorce.

"You okay, McPhee? It's none of my business..."

Sam was so absorbed in the letter that he scarcely looked up. "She's left with Roland." He tightened his grip on the knife.

The super was perspiring freely, and he wiped his face with a soiled handkerchief. Shock, regret, remorse... all these emotions and more were present in the super's eyes. Sam knew they were feelings he should be sharing.

Instead, wave after wave of sweet relief rolled over him. He just stood there leaning against the wall, feeling free. Free! Freer than he ever had!

SAM SAT DOWN on a park bench, so hungry he could hardly wait to devour the Chinese takeout he'd bought with the last of his pocket change. He was opening the cartons when a woman's voice came out of the night.

"You ain't going to last long here," she said.

The elderly woman's skin was darker than tar from the filth clinging to it, but her smile was bright enough to light up Pluto. She stood over Sam, regarding him with a cautious eye for a moment. She appeared to be out of breath. Her entire body lifted to meet each gasp.

"Is there something I can do for you?" Sam asked.

"I ain't had supper yet."

"And I hate eating alone," he said, flashing her a wide grin.

"The name's Queeny."

"Sam McPhee," he said. "Will you join me, Queeny?"

"You ain't crazy, are you?" she asked.

*"Me?"* It was summer, but Queeny looked like deepest winter. She wore a heavy wool coat and a hat loaded down with artificial flowers.

"You're lucky I ain't no loon," she said, grabbing at the carton of food he extended to her. She flopped down onto the bench and devoured the nourishment like a hungry wolf.

Minutes later, when she was reduced to licking her lips to savor the last morsel of the food, Queeny turned back to him. "You'd better come with me."

"I'll be okay," Sam replied.

"It won't cost you anything to admit you need help. You can't sleep here. It ain't safe in this park."

She was probably right. After all, this was her turf. Anyway, there wasn't any point in lying to her. "I don't have any money," he told her.

"Did I ask for any? Come along," Queeny said.

She was a small woman, not too tall, somewhat like a string bean inside a coat that could easily have housed a guest. She stuffed her hands in her pockets and led the way to the Potomac Boat Club.

"She's mine," Queeny said, pointing proudly to a single-masted twenty-foot yacht.

Sure. And he was Captain Hook. The neighborhood of yachts and shiny foreign cars seemed an unlikely place for a bag lady to live, but he trudged behind her, compelled by curiosity. The owners of the boat were probably vacationing in Florida. He followed Queeny aboard, half expecting the police to greet them. But only a ratty-looking cat met them at the cabin door. It curled around him, meowing and fussing as though it hadn't seen a human in weeks.

"Meet Lucky Pierre," Queeny said.

Inside, the overhead light winked weakly. A faint scent of cooking lingered. The compact cabin, though badly in need of repair, was tidy.

"Now then," she said, "you lie down. A little sleep sets your mind free and lets you think more clearly."

"Have you got any tools?" Sam asked.

"Whatever for?"

"I'll accept your hospitality if you'll accept my offer to make some repairs."

"I knew you was a decent man the minute I laid eyes on you. I had a son...just like you." She squeezed her eyes shut for an instant.

"It's the least I can do," he said.

"Rest now. I have an important errand to run," she said. "We haven't seen the last of each other, you and I."

# Chapter One

MacKenzie Ford felt a rush of excitement. Maybe because her father, Senator Anderson from Virginia, did not know that his law firm had hired her investigative services for this job.

Everything about her elusive father involved a little hocus-pocus like the way he'd disappeared when she was a child. If the senator had felt any remorse over walking out on the twelve-year-old Mack, after twenty years he had clearly gotten over it. Now he was completely absorbed in the hocus-pocus of his coveted elected position. He made Mack so angry that she'd never even used his surname, she preferred to use her mother's maiden name.

Mack crossed her legs to immobilize her jackhammer knee. Nerves always triggered the jerking. From the front seat of her Volvo, she looked through binoculars toward the boats moored at the

Potomac Boat Club. Mack was a headhunter for missing heirs. Now, she had four weeks to track down a missing beneficiary and acquire a deserted island from him. The part about the island raised goose bumps on her arms. The senator would move heaven and earth to find a deal. One characteristic Mack shared with her father was tenacity. She would move heaven and earth to find a rat.

Four weeks should be ample time to locate the missing beneficiary, one Sam McPhee. Mack had a passion for hide-and-seek. Perhaps McPhee would serve as a conduit to lead her to the machinations of a certain shameless senator.

She would nail the senator from the shadows, the same way he always swooped down on his innocent prey. *That's really what you're doing here, isn't it?* whispered a small, lost voice inside her. *Trying to hurt your father as badly as he hurt you.* She'd been Daddy's little girl until the morning he walked out the door for good, without a word....

Mack set the troubling thought aside and lifted the binoculars again. She had attracted the attention of a bum who was seated on the curb, leafing through a newspaper. That bothered her somewhat, since his piece of sidewalk happened to be directly in front of the *Phoenix*. But there was nothing she could do about him.

Or maybe there was. Mack slid out of her car and walked in the vagrant's direction. He lifted himself off the curb and started toward her, his long legs devouring the distance between them with powerful strides. Her attention was drawn at once to a body that had transformed baggy old clothes into an outfit befitting a swashbuckling pirate. The queue confining his dark, wavy hair exaggerated this impression.

Maybe he wasn't a bum. Maybe he was a poster model. And maybe he was an astronaut! Whatever he was, he couldn't be real. Real men never looked this good.

Several days' growth of whiskers covered his face, and dark sunglasses prevented her seeing his eyes. But she could read enough of his expression to know that she was being checked out, too. Which would have been acceptable, if not for the seductive grin tugging at his delicious mouth.

"Would you mind removing your sunglasses?" she asked.

For thirty-two years she had been looking for the man of her dreams, that rare man who knew exactly who he was and where he was going. Now, within her reach, he stood there, a time-traveling eighteenth-century pirate wearing shades. Perfect.

"No, ma'am," he said, in a husky murmur that straightened her spine and sent a hot, spiraling sensation through her stomach.

He made a production of removing his dark glasses, which he hung on the frayed pocket of his billowy white shirt. Then he studied her with the darkest, most intense eyes she'd ever seen. Experiencing a chill that the summer temperature could not justify, she questioned her judgment in confronting him. *Come on, Mack,* she told herself. *You're not going to let this hulking hunk intimidate you.*

Her head was bent back at an uncomfortable angle—and she stood five feet nine inches in bare feet. But this man easily topped six feet. His daring eyes broke away from hers to travel briefly over her body, causing a strange, languid heat to follow the path of his gaze.

"Excuse me?" she said, finding it difficult to concentrate under the scrutiny of his extraordinary eyes.

The usual lines and creases one would expect of a man in his thirties surrounded them. Early thirties, she figured, about her age. Her attention was focused on his face, which was uncomfortably close to hers. A strong jawline framed the most sensuous mouth she'd ever seen.

"Hello," he said smoothly, with a charm that was completely inappropriate under the circumstances. Mack had the sudden, uncomfortable sensation that he could divine her thoughts.

Instinct warned her to turn and run, but at the moment she lacked the desire to do anything but stand there, gaping at him.

"Cat got your tongue?" he asked, his sly grin revealing perfect teeth.

"No!"

She wasn't so much afraid of him—though he might be dangerous—as flustered by him, she thought sourly. And he seemed amused by it.

"I'm trying to find someone, and I'm at an absolute loss." Mack spoke rapidly, without taking a breath. She could hardly believe it was her babbling—without a trace of authority in her voice. She stumbled as she backed away, her face flaming. His hand reached out, as though to steady her.

"Careful," he said softly.

"I'm—I'm all right."

"That's good. I doubt I can be of any help to you," he said, running the tip of his tongue over his lips. "I'm not from around here."

She believed him. She'd never seen anyone like him anywhere—except in old pirate movies, where the pirate heroes were dangerously handsome and totally compelling. She wanted to appear cool and self-possessed, but inside, the sight of him set her aquiver. She'd always been a hopeless romantic, although at her age she supposed the condition could be considered delusional. Happily-ever-after only happened in the movies, she reminded herself.

"What's the party's name?" he asked, his dark eyes gleaming.

"What party?" she said, immediately realizing her mistake. Terrific. In a matter of minutes, a compelling, mysterious, fabulous-looking stranger had managed to turn a sensible, intelligent woman into a dumbfounded twit. She attempted to recover. "Oh. That party."

"What's the name?" he asked, all charm and persistence. His gray pants clung to his long legs from the force of the breeze that also made his white gypsy-style shirt billow sexily.

The wind was catching her from behind, wrapping her shoulder-length hair around her face. She could barely see through the blinding strands, but she managed to clear one eye to indulge herself with a breath-taking look at the tanned chest revealed by the V of his shirt. She did her best to ignore the sudden jolt of excitement that urged her to rip open his shirt and run her hands over his taut body.

"I can't help you if I don't know the name," he said.

"Name?" she echoed, staring at him as if she were hypnotized.

Too bad her idea of a worthwhile relationship entailed more than just great sex with a fabulous-looking man. When her gaze reached his mischievous eyes, he flashed her a mocking smile.

"Forgive me. I'm MacKenzie Ford," she said, extending her arm.

He reached for her fingers, and she felt a brief spark when their hands joined.

"Hello, MacKenzie Ford."

Mack withdrew her hand and hid it behind her back. She offered a nervous smile, one he neglected to return. It was just as well. She already felt as though she'd been hit by a comet. The electrical currents between them could have lit up the Las Vegas strip.

"I didn't get your name," she said.

"I didn't give it."

His answer was a cold reminder of what he was, and what she was doing here. She wondered why he was watching her so closely. Mack tossed her hair over her shoulder, trying to look casual. But there was something happening to her, something she couldn't have put a name to. And this alluring stranger was responsible.

"Are you all right?" he asked.

"I'm fine."

"You don't look fine."

The way he was looking at her was making her feel crazy. Out of control. Adventure lurked in his eyes. Everything about him appeared larger-than-life. With even the slightest encouragement, she would have set sail with this pirate and allowed their sexual chemistry to run rampant. The encounter had turned out to be a lousy idea, an unqualified mistake.

"Sorry I couldn't be of help," he said, sliding his dark glasses back on. "I've got to be going."

The next thing she knew, he was walking away.

"Wait!" she called after him. "I didn't tell you who I'm trying to find. His name is Sam McPhee. Do you know of him?"

He shrugged with the casual ease of someone who had nothing to lose and everything to gain. Like someone engaged in a relentless search for adventure. Just what she needed—a man on an endless quest for his next thrill.

"What are you, a process server?" After watching for her reaction, he laughed out loud. "I'm right, aren't I?"

Mack suffered a brief attack of paranoia. Was she so easy to read? Then her defenses bristled. She was a damn good private investigator. What did this guy, a derelict drifter who probably had no roots at all, know?

"Not exactly," she said, in a deliberately cryptic tone.

"I knew it."

Damn him! She recovered quickly, but he had already turned to leave. This time he was walking away for good. And she couldn't stop him. The realization shocked Mack back into the twenty-first century. She watched him vanish down the street— taking all her fantasies with him.

MACKENZIE FORD spelled trouble. Sam guessed that was part of her appeal. The sight of her stirred something inside him, something he hadn't felt in a very long time. He still felt surrounded by her presence, and he liked the feeling. Maybe a little too much. He doubted anyone had ever called her beautiful. In fact, he wondered why such a young woman looked so severe—straight, mousy brown hair streaked blond, round and overpowering glasses shielding serious pale blue eyes, like crystal ice cubes inside glass. Her slim, well-defined body sported dowdy clothes that were a departure from the designer brands his soon-to-be ex wore. That last thought had barely crossed his mind before another followed. No more women.

God! He couldn't believe he was feeling this irreverent. Queeny was dead. The first item on his agenda was a proper burial for her. In their last conversation, she'd detailed her wishes for a burial at sea, but the mortuary wouldn't release her body to him unless he could pay for their services. And that was where everything had stalled.

He heaved a sigh and walked the distance to the mortuary. Only a miracle would keep Queeny out of a pauper's grave. That Queeny deserved better was eating Sam up. The mortician had her on ice until he could come up with sufficient funds to cover his services.

As he stood in the casket room of the Chapel of the Chimes, Sam felt as if he were hooked up to an electric timer. *Patience. It takes patience. Get in a hurry and life will jerk you back.* Queeny's words of wisdom spoke to him inside his head—and his heart.

"I need time," Sam pleaded, pressing his fingers to his tired eyes. "Everyone has a right to a proper departure." And providing one for his friend happened to be the only way Sam could now repay Queeny's kindness to him.

"Time is a commodity. You can't expect me to grant it to you without defrayal," the mortician said, moving his shoulders in a way that reminded Sam of a rooster puffing out its chest after a conquest. "Mr. McPhee, you should understand that in order to dictate the terms, you must be on a paying basis. So far, that has not been the case."

The revolting little man with the pasty-colored skin appeared to be dangling from his uplifted, thinly drawn eyebrows. Sam was wondering how long he could successfully balance himself on the balls of his feet when, all at once, the man's brows came crashing down, as did his feet. "We have performed on our end. Your friend has been embalmed and turned out for the viewing, which is being held up for want of funding from you, Mr. McPhee," he said as once again his eyebrows jerked him skyward.

"A couple of days—"

"*Twenty-four hours.* Tomorrow I call the county to pick up the remains and dispose of them."

"You're too generous," Sam said, his tone deliberately sarcastic. "But, under the circumstances, I accept."

Under the circumstances, he had no choice. The man's pushiness was beginning to crowd him. Sam wheeled around and strode briskly to the front doors. Suddenly he needed fresh air. Lots of it.

Outside, he tried to steady his shaking hands. He unconsciously grasped his ring finger and twisted his wedding band, grateful it was still there. *Wedding band.* Mentally he repeated the words to himself, testing them, trying to connect them to something else, to something familiar. But the ring was just one more reminder of his prodigal wife. Impulsively he ripped off the ring and tossed it into the street.

"Good riddance!"

He moved down the sidewalk in the direction of the Potomac Boat Club, determined to come up with a solution to Queeny's dilemma.

After a few steps, his legs jerked his body to a halt. The ring! Of course! Dodging traffic, he darted into the street, frantically searching for the band. *Please, God, let it be there!* Brakes squealed, motorists cursed, and pedestrians gathered to stare at the crazy man. Had not the sunlight targeted the gold band, Sam might never have found it. "Thank you, God," he said, pocketing it.

He went around the corner and swung into a pawnship. The ring went for a hundred dollars. Money well spent, he informed the buyer, a huge smile lighting up his face.

He'd cleared the first hurdle. One more remained. The trickiest, most sensitive of them all— a burial at sea. The fact that he had precious little time eliminated a thorough consideration of his scheme.

He felt torn apart by something he did not recognize, a vital force strong enough to pull at his emotions and push aside his common sense. It became clear to him that he would do, at this point in his life, whatever he wanted to do. He knew stealing the body was unusual, but he wanted to set sail on the boat, and Queenie *had* wanted a burial at sea.

It seemed inconceivable, but why not try? First he would rent a U-Haul, and then...then he would indulge in a little body-snatching.

MACK STRAIGHTENED in the car seat and pressed the binoculars to her face. A barely perceptible tremor passed through her body as she saw a U-Haul truck back up to the *Phoenix*. Her eyes remained glued to the U-Haul rental, as if she expected it to speak to her, to explain its presence. The driver's door flew open, and she could make out a man jumping down from the cab. After a moment, she realized that he was striding toward her car. She reached for her cellular phone, in case she needed to call for help. For a moment she directed her gaze to the car seat to find it.

"Welcome to the neighborhood," said a deep, familiar voice.

Mack cried out, almost pitching the phone out the window.

"No need to be frightened," he said, amused by her reaction. "Remember me?"

Now she did. Even in the moonlight, she knew immediately that her pirate had returned.

"You *startled* me," she said, making a supreme effort to gather her scattered wits. "You did not frighten me."

He grinned generously, and Mack's heartbeat echoed in her ears as she watched a humorous gleam brighten his dark eyes. Her chest rose and fell with her breathing, and her damned knee had once again taken on a life of its own. She splayed one hand over it, hoping to settle it, but the vibration just moved up her arm until her entire body was shaking.

There was a tense silence, and then he said softly, "Alva sent you, didn't she?"

"No," Mack responded. *Be still,* she willed her knee.

"She took everything when she left. All I have are the clothes I'm wearing."

"I don't know who Alva is," Mack said, wondering how this Alva could have walked out on such a hunk of man. That question passed to make room for another: What was he doing with a U-Haul backed up to the *Phoenix?*

"Are you going to tell me what you want?" he asked, biting at his lower lip. "I don't much like sneaks."

"I'm not a sneak!" she protested.

"I don't like looking over my shoulder for you people."

*You people?* He had a strange fix on life. "Like I said, I don't know Alva, and I'm not a process server." Her leg was beating itself black-and-blue on the steering wheel.

His dark eyes registered confusion. "She took everything," he said, "except this." He displayed a Swiss army knife, that glistened under the moonlight. "Do you believe that?"

A knife? Wide-eyed, Mack shook her head. Okay. She had a certified lunatic on her hands. All the signs had been there, screaming at her. His appearance. His attitude. She should never, never have allowed him to get this close to her.

Her heart was pumping like a freight train, and her breath was coming quick and shallow. "This is a cellular phone," she said, displaying the technical wonder. "I'm one second away from calling for help unless you give me that knife and tell me who you are!"

"I'm SAM MCPHEE." Sam had a nightmarish vision of himself, handcuffed and being hauled away to jail. But the second he gave her his name, her attitude changed.

"*You?* You're Sam McPhee?"

Sam nodded. Despite her glasses, he caught the intensity of her eyes. He had frightened her and he felt bad about that. Somehow he didn't perceive her as the enemy—although he hadn't ruled out the possibility that she was the owner of the boat.

"Why didn't you tell me earlier?" she said.

"I thought you were a— Never mind." She looked edgy, as if she were lying—or afraid. His shabby appearance was sabotaging his credibility, and he felt a twinge of guilt for misleading her about his identity. But she was holding back, too. Until she came clean herself, she could assume what she wanted to about him. "What do you want with me?" he asked dryly.

"I have good news for you."

"Right," Sam said skeptically. Already kneeling down, he leaned forward and spoke in a deliberately husky voice. "You wouldn't tease me, would you?"

She started to protest, but he held up his hand to stop her. "Please continue."

If she was serious, perhaps he owed her an apology, but her simply showing up here had put him on red alert. At this point, he couldn't very well tell her that he was an attorney who had quit his job to have a go at the freewheeling life. Or that he'd grown weary of politics and corruption and three-piece suits. No. Definitely not. Maybe when he knew her better—and that was a very big *maybe*.

"I'll get right to the point," she said, sounding cool and self-possessed. "You've been named heir to Effie McQueen."

That got his attention. "I didn't think…she had an estate. Are you family?"

"No."

"A friend?"

"No, I'm here to make you a business offer on behalf of my client."

For the first time tonight, a smile illuminated her delicate face, which he could see clearly under the streetlight. It was fine-boned with a near-perfect shape. Her huge blue eyes gave her a vulnerable appearance, but Sam suspected there was a feisty side to MacKenzie Ford, too.

"A business offer?" he echoed, his words measured and draped with skepticism.

She nodded. "Effie McQueen named you as beneficiary of her trust."

"*Trust?* I don't understand. I traded her a little repair work on board the *Phoenix* for a place to lay my head." Sam's ability to remain calm had served him well when he practiced law. But those matters had not personally affected him. Nor had he been confronted with anyone compared with MacKenzie Ford. "Queeny only knew me for a couple of weeks. I assumed she had . . . limited assets."

"The McQueen trust was drawn up nearly thirty years ago. She needed only to insert your name as beneficiary. And, equally beneficial, the trust eliminates the necessity of probate. Now what all this means—"

"I know what it means. I just assumed she died intestate. Not that I wondered about her assets, but whatever she had—which was more than I would have thought she had—I assumed would go to the state." Shock hit him full-force, and he could only stare wordlessly. "How . . . how much?" he asked at last.

"There is no ready cash in the estate—just a small piece of property and the *Phoenix*."

"The *Phoenix*. I thought Queeny was a caretaker, or something like that."

MacKenzie Ford drew her hand up under her thick ponytail and flicked it off her collar. Her smile dazzled him, lighting up the night. It was the smile of a woman acting with confidence. Every inch of her was in control, challenging him.

"I have an offer that will allow you to keep a portion of the assets," she said with a certain charming persistence.

Her determination attracted Sam. "You've got my attention," he said, beginning to feel amused by everything as he attempted to digest what she was telling him. "I'm beginning to enjoy this."

"Good," she said, meeting his gaze straight on. Her voice was tinged with an odd nervousness. "I prefer to get right down to business."

He listened now without a single interruption, even curtailing his flirtatiousness. MacKenzie Ford gave her report in a straightforward, direct manner. She was a professional, he was certain of that. He wasn't any good at guessing women's ages, but she looked too young to be this savvy.

"There are taxes to be paid. You'll have to liquidate the estate to cover them," she said, deliberately avoiding the topic of his current financial status. "It's difficult to know how much, if anything, will remain."

"And you're the agent for this anonymous client who wants Queeny's property?"

"That's right."

She flushed. "I'm here to offer you a choice between a state land auction or the benefit of a private buyer who wishes to remain anonymous."

"Anonymous," Sam repeated, shaking his head. She was beginning to fascinate him. "Really. I suppose *benefit* is the operative word here."

"Not quite," she said. "*Tax* is more like it. In your case, there are tax liens on the real estate, and there are estate taxes. If you don't have the funds to pay them, your assets will be auctioned to raise the money. My buyer is offering to pay all the taxes in exchange for the real estate."

"Just like that?"

"Did I mention that you get to keep the *Phoenix?*"

"You must have overlooked that detail."

"It's all spelled out here in this contract I brought for you to read. Why don't you have a look at the papers?" she suggested, holding out the documents.

Alarms were going off in Sam's head. Someone with a lion's appetite was hungry for this real estate. It was only natural for him to want to know who and why.

"I'll want to see the property," he said.

"I'm prepared to charter Queeny's boat and pay you to sail us there."

"*Us?*"

"Yes, provided you know how to sail."

"Sure," he said.

She adjusted her glasses, and he noticed that her hand was shaking. Maybe she'd failed to consider that aspect of her offer—sailing off to God knows where with a complete stranger. Anything could happen.

"The *three* of us. I'm willing to pay for you to hire an additional hand—contingent on my approval, of course."

"I think you overestimate the space on board the *Phoenix,*" he said, exercising all his charm. "We'd be cramped . . . but I suppose we could manage."

"Good point," she said, apparently undaunted. But he hadn't missed the tiny, unexpected breath she had sucked in. He sent her a lazy grin to cover up his disappointment. He'd expected a reaction from her—hoped for one, actually—and that bothered him, considering the amount of time he'd known this woman. It was way too soon to want anything from her.

"There's a time frame involved with this offer. Once you've seen the island, I'm certain you'll be ready and able to make up your mind."

"Island?"

"Why, yes," she said with a rueful grin. "Didn't I mention that?"

"You probably overlooked it," he said, with a healthy amount of skepticism. By nature he was curious, and he didn't like surreptitious business deals. He wanted to know who her client was and what he wanted with an island.

"It's the last one of a series of barrier islands about twenty miles off the coast of Virginia in the Atlantic."

Tidal barrier islands were usually tiny by any standard. Flat, desolate, and uninhabitable. "Let me get this straight. You want to charter the Phoenix to sail *us* to *my* barrier island?"

"If that's agreeable to you. A chopper would be faster, but too expensive."

"No."

She tilted her head and looked at him curiously. "No?" she said.

He nodded, and she shot him a surprised glance.

"I'll call you," he drawled.

"Be reasonable, Mr. McPhee. I'm offering you a free trip to visit your property, as well as a cash buyer for it."

Sam rotated his shoulders. It was something he did when he was tired. "I'm just not into whirlwind tactics," he murmured, hoping he sounded convincing. Suddenly he was feeling a rush of adrenaline that had no outlet. MacKenzie Ford was the answer to his prayers, and he could hardly contain himself. He had an entire island on which to bury Queeny? Sam spun that information around inside his head, looking for the catch. And he figured MacKenzie Ford was it.

"If money doesn't carry any weight with you, what does?" she asked.

"Sentiment. But if I change my mind, I'll call you."

Sam winked at her and then wheeled around to leave. He could hear her sharp inhalation of breath as he strode across the street.

"But you don't have my number!"

"You haven't seen the last of me."

"I SHOULDN'T have underestimated him," Mack grumbled. "Well, not so fast, McPhee. I'm not through with you yet—not by a long shot."

The temptation to run after him was almost more than she could bear. It took every ounce of willpower at her command to keep from following him onto the boat. An odd sensation moved its way up her spine, raising the hairs on the back of her neck. *You've been alone too long,* she thought, realizing that the sight of this man who looked like a pirate had stirred up a wild blend of sexual chemistry, romantic love, and the almost-certainty that it wouldn't work.

Worse, Sam McPhee was the kind of sexy dreamer who intended to do whatever he wanted to do. Returning to the business at hand, Mack pushed aside the tantalizing thought of what his body would feel like pressed against hers in bed.

He wasn't making things easy, but Mack's determination remained undaunted. She was disappointed because he had failed to contribute a single clue to explain the senator's enthusiastic interest in the island. But once she visited it herself, she would be in a better position to puzzle out her father's sudden appetite for this particular piece of real estate.

Mack wasn't about to let Sam McPhee and his island slip through her fingers. She was determined to visit the place. But how in the world would she be able to pull off such a trip without Sam's boat and his help? The answer escaped her. She would just have to think her way around his obstinate nature.

When the solution came to her, Mack reached for her cellular phone to put the plan into place. Sam simply needed a different mind-set to make him receptive to her offer.

"There's a robbery in progress at the Potomac Boat Club—slip 27. He's driving a U-Haul truck. Hurry!"

# Chapter Two

"It was a dirty trick, throwing me in jail," Sam said from his cell. "And it's not going to work."

"There's something you should know about me," Mack said.

"What's that?" he asked.

"I never give up."

"Now you tell me," he said. "I've told these people who I am, and as soon as they check me out, I walk. I'm going straight back to the *Phoenix* to set sail for my island—alone."

"I don't want you in here permanently," Mack said, "but you need me to validate you as the legal owner of the *Phoenix*." Sam choked that down and continued to listen. "Unless I do, your visit here could turn into an extended stay. So here's how it's going to be. You give me your word that in the morning *we* set sail for the island, and I give the sergeant proof that you have legal title to the *Phoenix.*"

Sam splayed his hands against the bars to touch Mack's fingers. They felt soft, warm and definitely female. He allowed his fingertips to follow a leisurely path down her palms. Abruptly she broke away, bringing him to an unsettling state of awareness. The connection hadn't been broken. A red warning light flashed in his mind. She was like a drug to him, an indulgence he couldn't afford. He knew he would never get enough.

The best thing to do would be to kill the animal instinct inside him. But how? *Tough it out, Mc-Phee.* He looked into her serious eyes and wondered if she was hearing the same call of the wild that he was hearing. No. Dammit. She appeared to be in total control.

He considered the possibility of capitulating. He even considered telling her about his quest to bury Queeny, but he thought better of that notion. It was so unusual, she probably wouldn't believe him anyway. Why not come clean with her about himself? Sam had a pretty good idea of what she thought about him too, that he was a vagrant, a hobo... a nut. The trouble was, *he* wasn't certain who he was any longer. He needed time to sort things out. Regardless of who he had been, he didn't fit into that world any longer.

The island was sounding better and better.

The very idea of the two of them alone on the boat and the island fed his fantasies endless scenarios. The devil himself couldn't conjure up a more sadistic form of torture for him. Their bodies had been talking to each other from the moment they'd first met. And more than once he'd caught her looking at him with a puzzled expression in those pale blue eyes of hers. She was trying to figure out what made him tick, while he was trying to figure out why their bodies were so in tune.

*Don't even think about it,* he was warning himself, when the sudden appearance of a guard brought him up short.

"Time's up," the uniformed man said.

A decision was at hand, and it was his. Mack queried him with her eyes.

"Okay," Sam said. "You have my word."

Mack smiled her acknowledgment.

"You'll be well paid," she said, and left at the guard's urging.

Sam's relief was immediate, a feeling so strong he gained new strength from it. He swallowed and concentrated on the cool metal bars in his hands. Almost at once, a jailer appeared to free him from the holding tank. She'd kept her promise, he had to give her that. He was a firm believer in keeping promises.

"See you in the next lifetime," he called out to the rest of the inmates.

In a matter of minutes, Sam had collected his meager belongings and made his way to the outer lobby.

"Just in case you start to burn with nostalgia," the sergeant called after him, "we'll hold your reservation here open." The man laughed so hard that his entire body shook.

*Same to you, jerk.*

Sam ducked into the men's room. He splashed cold water on his face, hoping it would help to slow down his spiraling desire for Mackenzie Ford. The very idea of another relationship dredged up a myriad of emotions from a still-bitter place inside him. He dried his face with a paper towel, then tossed the towel into a trash can and exited the bathroom to set about finding her.

He didn't have to look far. He enthusiastically pushed open the glass doors to exit the compound and saw her waiting just outside for him.

"Need a lift?" she asked.

"No thanks," he said, breathing in freedom. "You've done enough for one evening."

In spite of his answer, he wanted to be with her, but he knew body-snatching would require his full attention. He kept walking.

"Wait a minute," she called after him. "How can I trust you to be there in the morning?"

"You can't."

"McPhee!"

"I gave you my word," he said without stopping. "What else do you want?"

"A guarantee."

*A guarantee?* He stopped abruptly.

"Okay," he said.

In half a second, he closed the distance between them and planted a hard kiss on her astonished mouth. He held her with an intimacy reserved for lovers, and she was clearly too shocked to resist. For a moment he felt her arch against him, felt her tongue stroke his. Her body was talking to his, sending messages to places he'd been out of touch with for too long. Sam was sending his own signals, even as he waged war with his animal instincts. *What have you done now, McPhee?*

He groaned and dragged his mouth away. "Damn," he murmured. Blood was coursing through his veins, making its own demands on his body. He could see the desire in her eyes, too, and it sent a sharp thrill rushing through his stomach. He struggled to get a grip on the situation. He'd only intended to kiss her, but this . . . He'd never in his life been turned on so fast, so intensely, or taken so high.

"Was that the kind of guarantee you had in mind?" he murmured.

Her recovery was complete and immediate, and there was no mistaking the sly smile on her lips.

She'd survived his incorrigible behavior with surprising resilience.

"If that's the best you can offer," she said, seemingly unmoved.

But Sam could feel the tension connecting the two of them. And he wanted to test it. "Do you feel cheated?" he said, a slight drawl stretching out his words.

Now anger glittered in her eyes. "Maybe," she said smoothly. "And maybe not. You don't always get a seat when you buy an airline ticket."

The round goes to the lady, he decided, edging backward. He figured that last remark was his cue to leave.

"Not so fast, McPhee!" she said, apparently having had enough.

"We'll get friendly later," he suggested, feigning more control than he actually felt.

He looked down at her and found that the moonlight was reflecting in her eyes, turning them a liquid blue. With a gentle hand, he brushed at the loose strands of hair falling against the side of her face. Touching her caused electrical currents to fire through him.

"Why didn't I shave?" he berated himself. "You'll have whisker burns."

"It won't work, McPhee." Her voice was as calm as the eye of a storm. "You can't distract me. Just be warned. If you're not at the Potomac Boat Club in the morning, on the *Phoenix,* I'll hunt you down.''

There was not an ounce of doubt in Sam's mind that he was a pawn in this business deal of hers, but at this stage there was little he could do about it. But he was curious, just the same. Who wanted Queeny's island, and why?

Then it came to him. The trip to the island presented a golden opportunity. He could seduce the information out of her during the cruise.

''That's what I like about you,'' he said, smiling sweetly. ''Tenacity... it's a trait we share.''

''I doubt we have anything in common, Mc-Phee.''

''You go after what you want—and you always get what you go after. So do I, Miss Ford. So do I.''

SAFE IN HER CAR, Mack touched her thoroughly kissed lips and was reminded of Sam's mouth moving on hers. The brief kiss had been a bold and swift reminder to her that she was a woman. But right now that was the least of her concerns. She had no choice but to follow Sam.

Twenty-four hours ago she wouldn't have believed it if someone had told her that she would find herself physically attracted to a drifter. She'd worked her entire adult life to build a secure world for herself. How stable could Sam be? And he was arrogant, flirtatious, reckless—and predictable. But she could tolerate thirty-six hours of him. The sailing would keep him occupied. Once they reached the island, a visual assessment was all she expected to accomplish. Then they could be on their way.

Mack eased her car onto the grounds of the boat club, parked around the corner from the *Phoenix* and turned off her lights. Over an hour passed before Sam showed up. Once he was inside the cabin, she continued to wait for the cabin lights to go out, an almost certain sign that he was in for the night. She was hot, tired, and hungry, and was eager to go home and pack for the trip.

Another hour passed, and she raised the glasses for one last look.

"I've been waiting for you," said a masculine voice through her open window.

Mack cried out, bouncing the binoculars off her nose.

Sam McPhee looked different. For one thing, he had changed clothes. For another, he'd bathed. She clamped her hand on top of her knee. All right. She'd been caught. She could handle this.

"You scared me," she said, willing calm into her voice.

Sam leaned inside her open window, supporting his weight on deeply tanned, well-muscled arms. The white undershirt he was wearing stretched tightly over his well-muscled torso.

"Back for more?" he asked, in a low, husky, deliberately teasing voice. "Are you always this enthusiastic?"

He wanted a reaction, and he wasn't going to get one. His eyes crinkled into a smile, and every one of Mack's professional instincts told her that this dark-haired enigma, who now offered her such a disarming grin, was trouble. But she hadn't come this far only to back down now.

"I've made you mad again," he said. "I'm sorry. I seem to have a talent for that."

"It's all right," she said. His grin was infectious, and she fought hard to hold back a friendly smile. "I probably deserved that for spying."

She couldn't believe her ears. Was she trying to be coy? Maybe, but for one blissful instant she was intimately in touch with every part of her body. She expected to turn to ooze any second and slide right onto the floorboards of the Volvo. All she could do was gape at him and hope he couldn't detect the fluttering of her heart.

"Mind if I get in?" he asked cautiously, his expression guarded.

Mack forced herself to relax. There wasn't anything personal about his suggestion. Besides, she did want to discuss the trip, and the supplies they would need. There would be time on the boat to question him about his knowledge of the island.

"Okay," she said. "But only for a minute."

"Thanks."

He strode around the front of the Volvo, and Mack allowed herself a sweeping appraisal of his luscious body. Once he was seated in the car, she could appreciate just how taut and muscled his legs were as they strained against a pair of tight-fitting Levi's. The outfit, completed by a formfitting white undershirt, was a distracting departure from what he had been wearing earlier.

"What should I call you?" he asked.

His shoulders were too wide for the bucket seat, and Mack stiffened to keep from touching him. He smelled of soap, and his hair looked darker—still wet from a shower, and slicked back into the familiar queue.

"Mack," she replied, feeling a curious anxiety.

"Okay, Mack."

"What do I call you?" she asked, needing a diversion from watching his full lips form her name.

"Sam," he supplied automatically while his eyes traveled over her body.

She followed his gaze, spellbound by his slow, careful appraisal. His tongue made a sweeping movement along the edge of his upper teeth. Every inch of her craved his touch. Her nerve endings were shorting out, and so were her thought processes.

"I didn't invite you inside my car to get friendly," she said. "We need to discuss the supplies necessary for the trip."

"Don't think you can drag civilization along. I don't intend to clutter up this little piece of paradise with any unnecessary garbage."

"Don't tell me you're one of those save-the-earth crazies."

"We could live without some technological wonders," he said.

"I'll bet you're one of those ozone-layer groupies, too," she said.

"No, but I could use a little space and fresh air."

"Personally, I'm dependent on the amenities," she said, feeling enough sexual electricity in the car to fry them both.

"What does Mr. Ford do to support your preferences?" Every time he smiled, his face turned into a series of strong lines and angles.

"I support myself," she said. "Not that it's any of your business, but there is no Mr. Ford."

*And what about Mrs. McPhee?* she wanted to ask. But she decided against showing that much interest in his personal life.

"Were you so certain I wouldn't be here in the morning?" he said.

She tried looking away, but his eyes, full of mischief, refused to be ignored.

"I wasn't going to take that chance. I couldn't be certain that you would leave a forwarding address," Mack answered softly, her lips curving into a smile.

"Let me get this straight. Do you always assume the worst about people?"

Sam was staring, clearly waiting for her reaction, and this time she was afraid she wasn't going to disappoint him.

"No. I just thought I had you figured out," she said, bluffing. "I never assume anything in this business."

For a moment she thought she detected hurt in his extraordinary eyes. She blinked, and when she looked again the teasing light had returned. He smiled at her in that sensuous way of his. "I want you to know you can depend on me. Go home and get some rest. I'll call you later as a show of good faith."

"Okay," she said, pausing to suck in a breath to clear her head. "You'll need this." She passed one of her business cards to him, inadvertently brushing his hand. She'd expected a response, but there was none. He accepted the card without so much as eye contact. A flicker of disappointment passed through her.

"We've just reached our first agreement," he said, his deep voice turning husky. "We set sail at seven bells tomorrow morning."

"I never get up before eight o'clock," she fired back. "And I can't have my groceries delivered before ten."

"This is great!" he said, enthusiastic as a child.

Satisfaction gleamed in his dark eyes as he lifted a hand to brush back a strand of hair that had escaped the confines of her ponytail. His touch left a trail of tingling flesh in its wake. Her instinct for self-preservation should have kicked automatically in at that point, but Mack had to jump-start it. He was looming ever closer.

"Why not spend the night?" he said in a near whisper.

Her breath caught, causing a tightening sensation in her abdomen. *Spend the night?* She should be throwing him out of the car, not entertaining his questionable intentions.

"That's not possible, McPhee," she said calmly. She had survived worse encounters with other men. But she hadn't been so powerfully drawn to any of them. Was that why he had kissed her? Had she been sending signals? And why was he deliberately taunting her?

"There's no hurry," he said. "We've got plenty of time to get acquainted."

*"What?"* she said, feeling even more self-conscious than she ever had before. The very thought of his mouth moving over the secret places of her body left her breathless and weak. But that

wasn't going to happen, because she wasn't going to allow it.

"We can finish this later," he said, flashing her a piratical smile.

She stiffened involuntarily. "There's nothing to finish. I'll have my supplies delivered to the boat in the morning. Now, if you don't mind, I'm in a bit of a hurry."

"I'll call you when you arrive home," he said smugly.

Rebuttal would be tedious and pointless in the face of such arrogance. So Mack simply watched as he turned to open the car door and ease himself out. She couldn't help but admire his easy stride as he moved around the Volvo. He stopped to lean in her window, balancing his weight on his arms while his hands hung freely inside, uncomfortably close to her.

"I think you're beginning to like me," he said.

She sighed. "Whatever gave you that idea?"

"We're a lot alike," he said. "Underneath it all, we're both looking for adventure."

His meaning was unmistakable, and so was his pirate's grin.

"I'm not looking for anything," she said, in her most professional tone.

"We'll see."

## Chapter Three

That kiss hadn't meant a damn thing to Sam. But he was certain he had felt Mack giving in to it. He had simply acted on impulse—something he was doing with a certain frequency these days. He could still taste her mouth, feel her softness. She hadn't deserved that monumental dose of arrogance from him. He had surprised even himself—and that was something else he was doing at a certain frequency.

It stood to reason, then, that he would do something crazy, like sailing away from reality to a deserted island with her. And that was exactly what he intended to do, come hell or high water. He'd called for a time-out in his life. How long it would last, he wasn't sure. He wasn't certain just exactly where Mack was going to fit in the scheme of things, either. For the time being, he figured, she knew all she needed to about him. He had his doubts about her forthrightness, too.

"The hell with D.C.," Sam muttered. Finally he was on the verge of escaping the world of nine-to-five businessmen in three-piece suits, married to their jobs, saving every dime they made for that dream house in the country.... He was sailing away to a deserted island! No smog. No honking horns. No muggers. No screaming telephones. No high-priced condos. Just a pristine piece of land....

He'd inherited a yacht, for heaven's sake. That detail was only now beginning to sink into his head. If only for the moment, the *Phoenix* was his. He intended to have the time of his life on this cruise. Nothing but sea breezes, salt water, and Mac-Kenzie Ford. But first he had to clear up another item on his private agenda.

Sam had forgotten all about Lucky Pierre, who was in the midst of sailing through the air in an effortless demonstration of levitation. Sam had no way of knowing whether the feline landed on his target or not, but he was on the kitchen table, making his presence—and his hunger—known.

"Chicken livers for dinner," Sam said with unabashed tenderness. He allowed his hand to glide gently over the animal's silky black fur. He stood watch until Lucky Pierre had licked up the last morsel of food, then he cleared the table and went to the porthole to check on Mack again.

She had finally left her post, freeing him up to accomplish his mission. He locked the cabin and walked out into the night air, thinking he would call Mack as soon as he returned. The U-Haul started on the first try, and he eased away from the boat club, not wanting to draw attention to the truck. He drove toward the Chapel of the Chimes, taking great care to abide by the speed limit.

After parking across the street from the mortuary, he settled in to wait. He watched from the cab of the U-Haul, his alert eyes piercing the night, waiting for the building to turn dark, an indication that it had emptied. He rolled down the truck window and breathed in fresh air to clear his head. Maybe he would feel better when he had Queeny safely stowed on the *Phoenix.*

He shifted his thoughts to the necessary tools. Again he took a mental inventory of what he had on board and what he needed to purchase: a shovel, rope, a couple of two-by-fours, hammer and nails, a small saw. He wanted to do this thing properly. It was a matter of pride. He owed Queeny a decent burial.

He waited for what seemed an eternity. The fatigue of the past few days had left him with adrenaline as his only fuel. Finally, when he looked up, the Chapel of the Chimes stood in darkness. It was on the minus side of midnight. It was now or never....

IN THE SAFETY of her apartment, Mack turned on her answering machine and relaxed. She'd be damned if she was just going to sit there waiting for Sam to call.

She could still feel the heat of his gaze burning into her. She had tried to remain businesslike under the scrutiny of his intense eyes, but she feared she had failed miserably. His presence still surrounded her. *There's no future in this,* the voice of caution warned, *there's only the moment. He's a time-traveler, Mack.* Maybe not in the literal sense, but he was a drifter. That was close enough.

All her life Mack had imagined herself with someone who could give her what had always been missing from her world—a happy home, security, someone to love. So why did she regret backing away from him? The sheer force of the attraction she was feeling for Sam scared the hell out of her, confused her. He was homeless, for God's sake. Was she crazy? And how could she have been so aroused?

Hot color crept back into her face. It had all happened so fast. But that was the way it was with men like Sam, she reminded herself. He would vanish just as quickly as he had appeared.

Mack checked the digital clock on her nightstand. Twelve-thirty. He wouldn't call now, it was too late. She hunched over her laptop computer and tried dialing up the credit bureau. Their terminals were down—had been all day—so she turned her attention to the recorder's office. She intended to check out the status of the property taxes on the island. Her tortoiseshell-framed glasses rested midway down her nose as she began studying the endless list of names.

Effie McQueen's name was right there where it was supposed to be, but what drew her attention to it was John Anderson's name. The senator had been paying the taxes on the island. He was less than thirty days away from becoming the legal owner of the land. Mack straightened up in bed and pushed her glasses closer to her eyes. Why the acquisition, when the island would be legally his in a matter of days?

There had to be a commonsense explanation for all this. She doubted he was trying to avoid publicity—unless, of course, he had something to hide. Right now she was too tired to puzzle it out. She attempted dialing up the credit bureau again, but their terminals were still down. If the police department hadn't turned up anything on Sam McPhee, there wasn't too much for her to worry about. She returned the laptop to her suitcase and padded into the kitchen for one last snack.

Back in bed, sinking her fork into a slice of chocolate cake, she felt her spirits rise. So what was it, she asked herself—euphoria from a sugar high, or the thought of Sam McPhee? She took another bite of cake, and was beginning to relax when the phone rang. She lifted the receiver and pressed it to her ear. Her hand was shaking.

"Mack?" Sam's voice practically oozed out of the telephone, slowly rolling into her ear and then down the rest of her body. The rush of adrenaline she felt caused her to suck in her breath. She recovered quickly, but not without a struggle. He was becoming adept at getting the better of her.

"Yes?" she said, trying to breath slowly to ease the pounding in her chest.

"I told you I'd call, and I always keep my word."

Mack raised herself up on one elbow. "I'd forgotten."

His laughter was immediate. "I think you were in bed, with the telephone close by, waiting for it to ring."

"You just never know about people," she mused.

"I told you I'd call," he repeated.

"I mean...you don't look like the type who honors commitments."

"When you get to know me, you'll realize that I always achieve what I set out to do."

"Overachievers are so tedious and boring." She hated men with an excess of macho pride. "I was hoping for a more...thrilling trip."

"Relax, Mack. The adventure hasn't even begun."

"Why did you call, Sam?"

There was silence at the other end of the line. "I wanted to hear your voice," he said at last.

Fearing that her voice would reveal her vulnerability, she just said, "Okay. Now that you've heard it, shall we say good-night?"

"Sleep well," Sam murmured.

"I always do," she said, but the dial tone was already buzzing in her ear. Damn him.

With the light still burning bright, Mack eased herself down into the comfort of her bed, thinking she was overdue for a new look, maybe a touch of makeup. She needed something to occupy her mind, which had turned on her, refusing to entertain any subject other than a tall, dark, handsome pirate....

MACK ARRIVED at 11:45 the next morning, over an hour late, and made no excuses for her tardiness.

"Hello," Sam said admiringly.

"Did my supplies arrive?" she asked, not making eye contact.

"They did indeed," he said. Something was different about Mack today. "Here, allow me to help you aboard."

"No, thank you, I can manage."

Against her objections, Sam grasped her by the waist to steady her as she climbed aboard. The step down wasn't steep, but that didn't matter. It was an

opportunity for him to touch her. Temptation demanded to have its way, and the few inches separating their bodies vanished when he lifted her next
to him. Resisting was out of the question. He swung
her around, intoxicated by her scent, his face so
close to hers that he could feel her breath.

"Put me down!" she demanded. "I'm not an
invalid!"

She held herself rigid in protest, but he kept her
in his arms for a long moment, savoring the softness of her breasts, the tautness of her slim legs.
Then he lazily lowered her body down the length of
his own to the deck.

"I have quite an effect on you, don't I?" he
mused, feeling the devil's prodding because of his
own arousal.

"None whatsoever," Mack said in a tight voice.

Maybe her head was sending that message, Sam
thought, but her body was telling him otherwise.
Her nipples had grown hard and erect underneath
her seductive stretch pullover top. A flush illuminated her fair skin, and her breathing had turned
shallow and rapid.

"Was this the kind of thrill you had in mind?"
he asked seductively.

She looked sexy and vibrant in white shorts and
the stretch top, both of which glided over narrow
hips. She might be thin, but all the right bumps and
curves were there—along with great muscle tone.

"I've had better," she said lightly, feigning control. "But I suppose it might be enough to satisfy a...desperate woman." She smiled wickedly. "I suspect you like your women desperate. It probably makes you feel safe. I'm afraid you'll find me boring, McPhee."

Another round to the lady, Sam realized. His plan of seduction had backfired on him. It was difficult to admit to such a strong attraction, considering the length of time he'd known Mack. But proof of it was the pang of arousal he felt as she smiled directly into his eyes. You've gone up against tougher opponents, he reminded himself. But he couldn't remember anyone quite like MacKenzie Ford. This wasn't going to be easy. She was no pushover.

"Those shorts are a mistake," he said, thinking that her fair skin was like an angel's.

"Haven't you ever heard of sunscreen?"

He had. But that wasn't the problem.

Her glasses were conspicuous by their absence and he saw eyes that were a bright, feverish blue. But there was something else different about her... Makeup. That was it. She hadn't worn any yesterday. Her features were better defined for the application, appearing more sophisticated. She'd been fastidious about her appearance, and Sam felt overwhelmed by the compliment she'd paid him. Mack's natural beauty stood on its own, but he couldn't deny how fabulous she looked this morning.

"You wanted me to notice, didn't you?" he said.

She turned away coyly before he could take a closer look. His interest was gaining momentum. Unable to help himself, he grinned.

"Come on, turn around and look at me so I can have a better look at your face. Hiding a little whisker burn?"

"No, but really, McPhee, if you're going to try to impress women with your romancing, you really ought to consider shaving first."

"I kind of like whiskers." He rubbed his face, which had a sly grin on it. "Don't you? They're supposed to bring out the animal instinct in women. And I like your makeup. It does something to me."

"Oh, really, McPhee," Mack moaned. "Don't you have some rigging to do, or sails to hoist? And let go of me."

But Sam hung on to her arm. With his free hand, he tipped his sunglasses down to make a closer inspection. She wasn't embarrassed and shy, and he was taking full advantage of it. *She should rip your heart out for this, McPhee.*

But this might be his only opportunity to get the upper hand with MacKenzie Ford, and he was doing just that, even at the risk of her despising him for it. Sam intended to employ every device he knew of to seduce Mack into divulging what she was holding back. He was going to get what he wanted. The voice of reason advised him to stop it while he could, before he did something he would regret. But it was too late to stop—much too late.

MACK DESPISED SAM MCPHEE, every inch of him, from head to toe, tight-fitting shorts included. She'd struggled to keep her expression blank when she caught sight of his muscular legs straining against his shorts. But her gaze had lingered as it slid upward, taking in everything—taut stomach, well-developed chest with a dusting of hair, broad shoulders. He'd probably left his shirt half-buttoned deliberately.

She hoped he hadn't noticed her obvious distraction. But she was prisoner to the sensations exploding inside her. Resistance had failed her again, the voice of her better judgment told her.

He could take his perfect body and time-travel right back to wherever it was he had come from. The man had to be a throwback to the Stone Age, if a little makeup impressed him so much. He had deliberately tried to embarrass her—and, worse, he'd succeeded. She cleared her throat and assumed an air of calm.

"Where should I put my duffel?" she asked as the ocean breeze freed wild strands of her hair from the confinement of her ponytail.

"Stow it below, in the cabin," he said lazily. "Down those steps and through the door."

If she'd expected this ill-mannered, pompous man to lend a helping hand, she would have been in for a wait. Of course, she didn't want his help anyway. Under no circumstances did she want to be indebted to him. Mack hoisted her bag and began the descent into the cabin, with Sam close behind her.

"Damn, that looks heavy," he said, giving the bag an exaggerated study through narrowed eyes. "What did you pack?"

"You wouldn't be interested," she replied as he squeezed by her to clear out a storage space for her bag.

She focused her gaze on the cabin floor, hoping he wouldn't notice her reaction to him. But surely he sensed her awareness. It was taking on a life of its own, responding to his nearness, his touch, his scent, shamelessly urging her to do the same.

And something else was drawing her, too, something on a different level. Something underneath Sam's arrogance. She recognized his flippant attitude as a defensive mechanism that kicked in to make him appear less vulnerable. She suspected there was a lot more to this man than met the eye. But how many times she could grit her teeth and bear his arrogant sexuality remained to be seen. And none of this altered her theory that men were not to be trusted—and especially not this particular one.

"Try me," Sam said in a seductive murmur.

"I didn't know you had a cat," Mack said, lowering her bag. "What's your name?" she asked the feline.

"Lucky Pierre," Sam said.

Lucky Pierre was curled in a tight little ball on top of an oblong box with a blanket thrown over it. The creature stood up and stretched, one leg at a time. Then, with characteristic feline grace, he descended from the box and made straight for her, stopping short and arching his back, puffing out his tail and prancing in a circle around her and her duffel.

"May I pet you, Lucky Pierre?" she asked, reaching out to soothe the black cat, who had already turned on his motor. He rubbed against her legs, purring. Mack reached down to stroke his head, then picked up the contented animal. He licked the back of her hand with his sandpaper-rough tongue. "What's that?" she asked, pointing to the oblong plywood box Lucky Pierre had been napping on.

"Gear," Sam said, without missing a beat. "You know...flares, life jackets, the usual."

He was looking at the box as if something vitally important were inside. Had he told her it contained a cache of guns, she wouldn't have been surprised.

"Shall I fit you with a life jacket?"

He grinned at her. It was a pirate's grin—less than honorable, and wickedly enticing. The suggestion brought Mack's gaze back to his.

"You can do better than that, McPhee," she quipped. "But since I know where they're stored, I can fetch one myself."

"Check with me first. I have the key."

"You keep it *locked?*"

"I don't know anything about you yet, do I?" he said, with an innocent expression. "But we're going to change all that."

Mack glared at him, then crawled over the box to reach a porthole.

"Leave the portholes fastened down," Sam cautioned. "We'll be shoving off soon."

"Aye, aye, Captain," she said with a mock salute. "I was just thinking about a little fresh air to help me get my sea legs."

Mack knew damn well that her shakiness had nothing to do with acquiring her sea legs. It was the sheer physical strength and sexiness of this broad-shouldered man in the tight shorts that had her intoxicated, dizzy.

"Come topside after you've stowed your gear. I can use an extra hand."

"Sorry," she said, momentarily startled. "I don't know a thing about sailing."

Her stomach was fluttering, and they hadn't even left the dock yet. For the next thirty-six hours, she would be confined on this yacht with him. She was determined to keep her distance.

"Perfect," he said, leaning nonchalantly against the door frame. It was difficult to meet his gaze head-on, but the alternative was equally unsettling. If she wasn't locking gazes with him, her eyes were following the contour of his body.

With deliberate ease, he ran his tongue across the edge of his teeth. "No bad habits to break," he explained, moving toward her with enough momentum to convince her that he had something in mind.

"Coming from you, that sounds strange." She struggled to remain unmoved. No point in allowing a display of anxiety for him to gloat over. That was what he wanted—to drive her crazy with his wicked charm. Unfortunately, she suspected her own desire would push her over the edge first. "I figured you to be a nonconformist," she said in a husky voice.

Sam stopped just short of pressing his body against hers. His hand came up to push the loose hairs away from her neck. Spirals were shooting through her stomach from the feeling of his skin against hers. His gaze seemed to penetrate the depths of her soul, probing, searching for the truth.

Apparently made confident by what he saw there he casually lowered his head and pressed his lips against her neck. The action was deliberate and taunting, and Mack was helpless to protect herself.

"That's only because you don't know me yet," he said, cupping her face with his hands. "But you will..."

MACK KNEW perfectly well that Sam wanted to goad her, to keep her on the defensive. She was reminded of her reasons for tagging along on this cruise. How difficult could it be to stay out of Sam's way? She was MacKenzie Ford, unbending, unyielding, tough....

And who was Sam McPhee anyway? Just the most pigheaded man she'd ever met in her life. But that aspect of his personality she could deal with. It was the beguiling, charming part of him that had red-hot desire running rampant through her body. Mack gritted her teeth for the umpteenth time in less than an hour.

Somehow she had to divert his intense sensual pull. Every time they made contact, her reason short-circuited. She turned her attention to the endless ways she could make his life miserable, but realized that she needed to learn more about him in order to do so. She had some unfinished investigative work left, and the credit bureau topped her list.

She ducked into the bathroom and popped out her contact lenses, questioning her reasons for having worn them in the first place. The boat lurched, and she was tossed against the wall. At least they were finally under way. Tending the boat ought to keep McPhee occupied for the time being. She slipped her glasses on, ready to do battle.

Her first serious assessment of the area showed her that it was larger than she had anticipated. And tidier. She had been expecting dust, and dirty clothes tossed all over the place. A normal preconception about a man who had apparently lived on the streets, she thought.

The large living area surprised her, too, even though it was just one room with a private bathroom attached. In fact, the outward appearance of the *Phoenix* had fooled her. While there was very little deck space topside, the galley, sleeping quarters and bathroom were more than adequate. *Think of it as a vacation,* she thought. To that end, she had ordered every gourmet food available in a can.

A black streak whizzed by her, landing on the box. Amused, she strolled over to stroke the cat.

"Are you nervous, too, Lucky Pierre?" The feline rolled over so that Mack could scratch his belly. "So tell me, what do you know about this Sam McPhee?" Lucky Pierre buzzed with contentment. "Why don't I pull out my laptop and see what I can find out about him?'' The cat slapped at her scratching hand. "No offense intended.''

This excursion would be a lot easier if she could glean Sam's history. He was complicated, she knew that. And he was smart. Very smart. Which she liked. Everything else appeared to be a contradiction. Her laptop computer was in her bag, as was her cellular phone. In five minutes she could track every major decision in Sam's life for the previous ten years.

She moved quickly to extract the technological wonders. The moment Sam came below, she intended to go topside. She hooked up the phone to the computer using her adaptor, grateful now that she had paid the extra money for the internal modem.

Her fingers froze in position when a sudden noise filtered down the stairs and into the cabin.

"McPhee? Is that you?''

She waited, holding her breath to block her panic.

## Chapter Four

"At your service," Sam drawled from the doorway.

He smiled at Mack, and her attraction to him started all over again. He was sweeping her off her feet by pushing against her boundaries. Each time he crowded her, she felt the electricity, the devastating force of his pull. It was as though an adventure were at hand. She could no longer deny that she longed for adventure—longed to walk on the wild side of life while she was still young enough to throw caution to the winds.

"Are you chilly?"

At the sound of his voice, she blinked herself out of her private world and was surprised to feel herself shaking.

"Do I have that kind of effect on you?"

Mack's anger was instantaneous. "That's your trouble, McPhee," she said through gritted teeth. "Your ego is devouring your brain."

He countered by flashing her a grin so enticing that it made her want to step over the invisible line separating them. *Take a deep breath, MacKenzie.* There was no point in longing for something that was ridiculous and impossible.

"We'll fight this thing together," he murmured, obviously pleased with himself. "We won't let it get out of control." He paused to scrutinize her. "You're okay, aren't you?"

"No," she mumbled. Her body was shaking—or was it her insides? The man got to her. She didn't know how to deal with him yet, but she was working on it. "I'm not okay, and I won't be until this adventure is over with."

"Did you say adventure?"

"That's the other problem you have. You don't know how to listen."

"Mmm... what are you doing with that blanket in your hands?"

An uneasy feeling spilled through her. She turned around and tossed the blanket over her laptop and her cellular phone, as calmly as if she were making up a bed.

"Just thought I'd throw on an extra cover in case it gets damp and cold tonight."

"You might have asked first," he said. The words sounded almost like a reprimand.

"If I had known a blanket would be so important to you, I would have."

"I keep that blanket there for Lucky Pierre."

"Aye, aye, Captain," she said, easing away from her berth to head for the stairs.

Sam blocked her way. For a moment he didn't say a word. He just stood there, leaning back against the door frame, with his muscled arms wound together and his powerful legs crossed at the ankles. She didn't know what was on his mind, but something definitely was. The man was always scheming.

"What's your hurry?" he asked lazily.

"No hurry." *Liar.* She had to get out of here before there was a meltdown. Her breath caught in her throat, and for a moment she had to remind herself to breathe. "I just need some fresh air. And you need an extra hand."

There was a sudden silence in the cabin. His bold glance strayed to her breasts, and Mack regretted having chosen to wear the stretch top. She knew a moment of panic as she felt his eyes devouring her. She had just put out to sea with a total stranger who might decide to demand God alone knows what for her safe return. On the other hand, what was he going to do? Throw her onto a bunk and make wild, passionate love to her? It didn't seem likely.

"Get out of my way," she said.

"Better put on some sunscreen," he warned.

"I never burn," she said, smiling sweetly and pushing past him.

"I wouldn't count on it," he murmured.

She found sailing surprisingly exhilarating. There wasn't much room to move around on deck, but the open expanse around her gave her a much-needed sense of freedom.

The sails flapped loosely in the wind, as though they might come apart at any moment. "Everything okay?" she called out as Sam busied himself with the sheets of cloth that powered the yacht. The deftness of his hands surprised and relieved her. She was glad they had something else to challenge them besides her, and that she could rest easy—at least for the moment.

"Just preparing to set sail," he said, hauling the mainsail to port.

The strength of his body was commanding. His shorts allowed Mack the opportunity to absorb the full impact of his powerful legs.

"What can I do?" she asked, hoping the shakiness in her voice wouldn't be carried to him on the wind.

"Want to tackle the jib?"

"Can I?"

"I don't know," he said, with that pirate's smile that only he could deliver. "Can you?"

His lips twitched in amusement, but she failed to appreciate his humor. "Just show me the jib," she said, feeling awkward and unusually self-conscious, "and tell me what to do."

"As soon as I finish with this mainsail," he said. He looked devastatingly handsome against the vast blue sky. "Then we'll see what you're worth."

The movement of the boat through the waves seemed to rock Mack, to mesmerize her, as she watched Sam work. Whatever it was he was doing, he performed the task with speed and efficiency.

"See that smaller sail flying next to the mainsail?" he said.

She nodded.

"You're going to work it while I manage the larger sail. Don't worry, you can handle it."

His tone only served to reinforce her determination to succeed. His condescension was undoubtedly revenge for her having landed him in jail. Of course he would seek retribution. He wanted a reaction from her, even if it meant embarrassing, harassing and humiliating her. And she intended to play along until she saw a chance to turn the tables on him.

"Slacken off the jib to starboard with that rope," he called out. "The one at your feet."

As she absorbed another onslaught of sensation at the mere sound of his voice, she realized she had failed to factor in the chemistry between them. All she had to do was brace herself against his presence. She was determined to stand her ground. While her hair tangled in the wind that whipped about her, her hands curled around the jib rope.

"Do you know your starboard side?" he asked, his tone and expression challenging her.

"Of course I do," she snapped, meeting his gaze defiantly.

"All right, then," he said. "Loosen the jib rope at your feet, to your starboard side."

His shirt billowed in the wind, revealing a near-perfect body. Mack indulged herself while she performed the task. His stomach was tanned and tight, and she wondered if his street attire had been some sort of disguise. Masquerading as a vagrant? With that body? She didn't think so.

"That's enough," he said. "Now wrap the rope around that hook until it's secure."

"Aye, aye, Captain."

"Well done," he said, in the first approving tone she'd ever heard from him. "Well done indeed."

The sail and the jib filled up all at once, propelling the *Phoenix* forward with enough force to send Mack flying into Sam's arms.

"Whoa . . . Where you headed in such a hurry?" he said, his voice deep and sexy.

"Damn you," she breathed. "You knew that was going to happen. Why didn't you warn me?"

"You like to be warned, do you? Well, here's a warning—you're about to be kissed."

Mack stared at him in complete astonishment. "You wouldn't," she challenged.

"Oh, but I would...."

SAM WAS NOT going to stop until he had succeeded in breaking down Mack's defenses. Trouble was, he didn't know whose were actually crumbling faster—hers or his. Driven by frustration, he covered her lips and thrust his tongue into the deepest recesses of her mouth, still wanting more...much more.

There was no room for her to retreat except into the railing, and the more she squirmed against him, the harder he pressed his hips against hers. He'd intended to melt her defenses, but he was the one who was turning to warm butter. After what seemed like a small eternity, he broke the kiss.

"Really, McPhee..." The words came shakily from Mack's swollen lips. "You're so predictable."

Had she looked down, she would have noticed just how predictable. She was no longer struggling to free herself, or to break the embrace. The only obvious sign of resistance to him was the stiffness in her rigid body. Sam ran his fingers up her spine toward her neck, and an audible gasp escaped her.

"What makes you think so?" he murmured, and then kissed her again.

She struggled wildly, twisting her head from side to side to free her mouth from his, digging her fingers into his shoulders. The more she thrust her hips about, the more his arousal demanded.

He was about to break the kiss again when her mouth slackened to accommodate his probing tongue. Her sudden passion took him totally by surprise. His every sense was riveted on the arms locking around him. She arched against him, tugging impatiently at his body while she moved invitingly against him. He hadn't planned on this reaction from her. He had to get a grip on the situation.

He groaned as he reluctantly pulled away. Mack gasped, sinking against him in a way he had dreamed about. He cleared his throat in a feeble attempt to buy time to steady his ragged breathing.

"You catch on quick," he said, surprised at the shakiness in his voice. Then he gave Mack a wink and a blazing smile before indulging her hot, wet mouth yet again.

WHAT WAS SHE going to do now? Mack wondered. She had used the same physical weapons on him that he had on her, intending to knock him down a few notches. Instead, her resistance had turned to ooze before his very eyes.

And now one of her hands was curled around the back of his neck, urging him closer. Even through their layers of clothing, she could feel his throbbing arousal. Involuntarily she tightened her knees, embracing him with her legs. Then he was pushing up her top to free her protruding breasts. She arched them to meet his kneading palms. She heard a sigh, and realized it was coming from her, though she felt too weak to make a sound. He could take her with very little effort, she realized dimly, and she would urge him on.

"Sam...don't..." she managed to gasp.

God! She had to put an end to this. She pushed against his powerful body until there was at least a little distance between them. Breathless, she squeezed her eyes shut and attempted to rearrange her top.

She ran her fingers through her tangled curls. The humidity had already made the straight strands wavy, and thicker than usual, and she knew she probably looked like Little Orphan Annie. The wet, salty breeze caressed her face, and she welcomed the sensation as she tried to figure out a way to make a graceful exit.

"Don't bother primping for me," Sam said smoothly, his tone exuding confidence. "I'm into the natural look."

"*Primitive* is more like it," she said lightly, grateful that her voice sounded almost normal. She headed for the hatch, her heart beating as though she'd just escaped with her life.

"You're not leaving so soon—just when we were getting friendly?" Sam drawled, flashing that smile of his.

*Friendly?* Mack stopped and held herself completely still—except for her chest, which rose and fell in quick, short movements. She knew all about men like Sam McPhee. Charming, elusive, and full of hocus-pocus.

"Thank you for an interesting afternoon," she said, her voice as smooth as syrup. "I'm going below now."

"If I can be of any assistance to you, I'd be happy to oblige."

"You're being paid to sail me to an island, McPhee," Mack said tightly. "That's what you can do."

"You know what your trouble is?" Sam said, his tone oozing feigned concern. "You don't know how to have fun. You should cut loose. Live a little."

"What you do with your free time is your business, but for the time being, you're in my employ. We made a bargain, remember? At the moment, you have no real proof of title to the *Phoenix*."

"Nor do you," he murmured.

Alarm swept through Mack. She hadn't counted on his standing his ground with her, almost mocking her. He had called her bluff.

She felt him move closer, and just when she thought he was going to put his arms around her, he pressed his hands against the railing on either side of her, trapping her between them. She locked gazes with him, matching arrogance with arrogance.

"What do you want?" she asked him, her tone cold and flat.

"What do you think I want?" he asked softly, his mouth so close to hers that she could almost taste it.

"You haven't answered me," she said dryly.

"You haven't told me what you're offering."

Mack's heart was beginning to pound, but her mind warned her not to swallow the bait. His expression told her he wanted much more than just a daring kiss. Despite her mind's warning, she felt herself caught in the intensity of his gaze, and knew beyond a doubt that sooner or later he meant to have his way.

As MACK GLARED up at him brazenly, Sam became aware of just how pale blue her eyes were. They blazed with such an intensity that he was taken aback. He removed his hands from the rail, relinquishing any chance of feeling again those inviting lips, that smooth, fair skin that tempted his hands, and those soft mounds, with their protruding nipples, that he'd felt earlier.

For a moment Mack didn't budge. She stood there staring up at him, rage flashing in her eyes. But in spite of her outrage, there was a passion in the depths of her gaze that he had seen in no other woman's eyes.

"Get out of my way!" she said.

"Did I do something to offend you?" he asked in a silky-smooth voice. "I thought you were enjoying yourself."

"Think again, McPhee."

Nice going, Sam told himself. His plan of seduction had been flawed by one major miscalculation. His own desire had rushed him. His grand scheme had left his heart beating too fast and his breathing too ragged—not to mention the painful throbbing sensation between his legs. He hadn't counted on Mack charming *him* with her uninhibited passion, disarming him with the most powerful kiss he'd ever received, and then calmly walking away.

He was shaken, but not defeated, and he meant to keep at it until he found out what he wanted to know. His anonymity carried with it intriguing possibilities. Besides keeping Mack off guard, it freed him to be whatever he wanted to be, to do whatever he wanted to do. He meant to figure out what Mack was involved in and who the buyer for the island was, and he would attempt to elicit that information from her by charming her in every way he knew how.

MACK GLANCED around her tiny quarters, trying to ignore the pricking of her conscience. She refused to entertain the possibility of becoming involved with Sam McPhee. She didn't even like the man.

She had spent most of the afternoon fighting the renewal of feelings she had long resisted. Was she so easy to read? Her pride bristled at the thought, and she fetched one of the miniature bottles of brandy she'd had delivered for the trip. She twisted off the cap and tipped it to her lips, drinking enough to bring on a coughing fit. Still, it felt warm and friendly going down, like an old friend, intimate and trustworthy.

A riot of confused emotions battled within her. She acknowledged her attraction for this enigmatic, arrogant man. Under different circumstances, she might have entertained the idea of striking up a relationship with him. She'd kissed him as she had never kissed another man. There had been other kisses, other encounters, but none that had brought on such a response from her. Sam McPhee was a man who could make her senses reel and ignite her passions on a moment's notice. Again the voice of warning rang out loud and clear.

Sam acted like the sort of man who lived for the moment, and impulsive behavior was not what she was looking for in a man. She was a disciplined woman. A professional. He had probably never held a steady job in his life. Just look at his bronzed body, she thought. He could be a beach bum. He even ran around barefoot.

*Passionate?* Had he called her that? He obviously wasn't aware that she had long been celibate. Nor would he be—not if she could help it. Sam McPhee was becoming a constant, sinful craving for her, one she was constantly trying to control. Just the thought of his body rubbing against hers shot a pulsing shiver through her. What a fool she'd been to put her life in the hands of someone like him—someone who lived for the moment, someone impulsive, someone who probably had no roots at all.

How could she be feeling this kind of attraction for a complete enigma, a homeless man? Everything about him was off the charts in the risk department. And she wasn't into taking risks.

She ran a tongue over her swollen lips, feeling confused, unable to believe what had just happened. Oh, not Sam kissing her. That didn't surprise her. What shocked and scared her was what *she* had done. She had kissed him back. In a matter of seconds, her passion had intensified to a boil, had nearly gone out of control.

The logical part of her brain demanded answers. Unfortunately, she could come up with none. The important thing, Mack assured herself, was that she had made it through what she was counting on being her first and last kiss with him. Then, when she'd seen no other way out, she'd retreated.

But that was the trouble. She'd lost ground. The only way to gain it back was to throw Sam off guard. She couldn't have him thinking that all he had to do to get what he wanted was plant a kiss on her unsuspecting mouth. But then, maybe it would be best to put the whole incident behind her. After all, this trip would be over in slightly more than twenty-four hours. And then she would never have to see Sam McPhee again. Ever!

She helped herself to another brandy to calm her nerves. She squeezed by Lucky Pierre's box and wondered why men were always berating woman about what they carried around with them. For a transient, he lugged a cumbersome load. She considered taking a peek, but changed her mind when she spotted the morning newspaper that had been delivered with her groceries. She grabbed it and made her way back to her bunk, where Lucky Pierre was sleeping soundly.

On the front page was a small article on Senator John Anderson, reporting on his recent vow to clean up the mounting garbage problem in Virginia. *Garbage?* For a moment Mack allowed the information to float around the investigative part of her brain. A major piece of the puzzle fell into place, and at some point Mack knew she was going to have to level with Sam.

She jumped when Lucky Pierre lurched to his feet. The cat's body stiffened, and his toes contracted. His eyes opened wide, and his ears pointed toward the cabin stairs. He bolted to the end of the berth and stood there, waiting. A second later, Sam appeared, looking handsome with his thick hair falling, wind-tossed, over his forehead.

Mack's instincts went on red alert.

## Chapter Five

"There's a storm building northwest of us," Sam said, forcing the concern out of his voice to avoid upsetting her.

"Who's tending the wheel?" Mack asked with a wan smile.

"We're adrift for the moment." Her worried expression made him explain. "We're in calm water. The sails are down and we're changing over to engine power. But the ride is likely to turn rough—especially topside."

"Thanks for the warning, Captain," Mack said, deliberately avoiding eye contact.

She stood up, and Lucky Pierre promptly jumped on top of Queeny's box.

"Don't do that," he warned the contrary feline, casting a reprimanding glance the cat's way.

"Don't do what?" Mack asked.

"Don't . . . let Lucky Pierre bother you."

Sam caught himself. Mack was going to find out about Queeny's body eventually, but telling her now might make her too suspicious to confide in him. He couldn't expect her to understand that he had just done something on impulse, and he couldn't expect her to understand the debt he felt he owed Queeny. Lord knew she probably thought he was crazy already. Besides, if she could have her secrets for the moment, so could he.

"Oh, he's no trouble at all," she answered.

"See that you're not, Lucky Pierre," he said.

Sam watched in horror as Mack sauntered over to the box to pet the feline. She propped her head up with her arms balanced on the top of the make-shift coffin and just stood there gazing at the cat.

Sam pulled Mack next to him so quickly that she gasped, startled. She already considered him impossibly fresh. This sort of behavior from him would require no explanation.

Getting his hands on Mack wasn't exactly a dreaded chore, but this time his intention was to treat her as a lady, with care and respect. But Mack didn't know that. She squirmed out of his grip.

"You'll need a jacket," Sam said with a half smile. He released her and shrugged out of his. "Here..."

"Really, McPhee, I know how to take care of myself."

She wasn't particularly friendly, and she wasn't at all flirtatious, but she didn't back away, either. He wrapped her inside his windbreaker, feeling her body heat burning through the thin fabric of his jacket. The galley suddenly felt smaller. Sam stared at Mack for a long, calculated moment.

"The wind tends to get chilly as it blows across the water," he murmured, allowing his hands to linger on her shoulders.

Even as he covered her, he felt her body trembling. Sam allowed a finger to caress her neck. He searched her face for a reaction. Her phenomenal pale blue eyes were as round as saucers, and filled with trepidation—or was it desire?

"You're afraid of me...aren't you?" Sam said, testing her ire.

"Far from it," she mumbled, looking away. "I'm sorry to spoil your fun by my lack of enthusiasm."

Sam knew what he had felt going on with her trembling body and her rapid pulse as he'd helped her slip into the jacket. There had been no lack of enthusiasm.

"I've made you angry," he said.

"No, McPhee," she said through gritted teeth, "you have not."

"Did you know that anger is just another dimension of passion?"

The boat tilted before Mack could answer. The swift action pitched Mack into his arms.

"I'm tried of playing games, McPhee," she said.

"Easy," he said soothingly. "There's no reason why we can't be civilized about this."

"Go away," she said in a bored voice.

"I should have warned you that when I want to do something, I just do it."

"I'm sure you do," she said. "Now let go of me," she warned, tugging at his arm.

His lips touched the top of her head, and she gradually ceased to fight him. He breathed in the fragrance of her hair. There was the freshness of the salt air in it, and something else, a smoothness he could only liken to silk. He wanted to pull her to him, but at the same time he feared breaking the magic spell that had descended on them.

Finally, he couldn't hold back any longer, and he pulled her closer. Mack attempted to wriggle away to escape his intimate touch.

"I have quite an effect on you, don't I?"

Fire was building in her eyes, the kind of fire that could set a man's soul ablaze. "No," she lied. "You don't."

"Yes, I do," he said, grinning and pressing her body against the length of his. "You like me." He bent his head down until only a breath separated their lips. "You like me a lot."

"I hate you," she said calmly.

He nuzzled the pulse at her throat, feeling it race beneath his touch. He hadn't intended to go this far with his teasing, but as it became clear that she thought he wouldn't stop short of kissing her, he allowed the deceit to continue. He wanted her, wanted to feel her skin warm beneath his hands. He could already feel her passion building, and anticipation drove him to the edge. This time he had serious doubts about whether he could pull away.

When his lips claimed hers, the fight she put up was not convincing. He deepened his kiss, probing with his tongue for a response. It came with a little moan as she offered her mouth to his, yielding to his embrace.

Sam's passion rose to heights he had never known. His hands turned feverish and traveled swiftly and knowingly to the soft mounds protruding against his chest.

"Stop it," she said. "I don't want to be involved with you."

"Yes, you do," he murmured, his arousal demanding more. "You just won't admit it."

"Go away!" she said, pushing his hands away and writhing free of him.

He winked at her. "Your problem is that you need to loosen up and live a little."

"You're despicable."

"I kind of like you, too," he said, reluctantly drawing away to study her. "No point in fighting this. We're at the mercy of the Fates."

He widened his grin, in a feeble attempt to appear in control. In truth, his senses were reeling from the contradictory messages being sent. One minute Mack was returning his kiss with more hunger and feeling than he'd ever longed for, the next moment she was pushing him away as though all that passion weren't real.

"I hope you fall over the rail and take that silly grin with you," she snapped.

Maybe she had a point. A little dip would definitely serve to cool him down. Where was all this taking him?

"Hold that thought," Sam said. "I've got to check topside. We'll figure out what to do about your problem after dinner."

"What problem?"

"You're a hot-blooded woman, MacKenzie. Sooner or later we're going to make love and satisfy your cravings."

Mack just stood there openmouthed, gaping at him in shock. "You make too much of yourself," she said once she'd recovered enough to speak. "Why would I want you to make love to me, when I can't even stand to have you touch me?"

"We'll see," he said, bending his head until his lips nearly touched hers again. "You're excitable, you know that?'' Fiery anger replaced the overwhelming hunger he had seen in her eyes. ''I like feisty women.''

She had almost succumbed again, almost fallen into his arms again, but now wrestled herself free.

''Get out!'' she ordered, pointing to the hatch.

''Are you going to fix dinner?'' Sam asked as innocently as a hungry puppy.

Luckily, he was nearly topside when he heard the breaking glass.

MACK'S WORST FEAR had been realized. Sam had absorbed her fantasy. Now it was real. She wanted to deny her desire for him, but no matter what happened, she knew she wanted more each time she saw him.

She spread newspaper on the floor and swept the broken glass onto it. She felt like a rat with a capital *R,* but it was too soon to tell him about the senator's planned dump site. He might just turn the *Phoenix* around and head back to Washington.

The situation was becoming impossible. Mack wasn't going to allow herself to become involved with Sam, no matter how tempting the prospect might be. She wouldn't allow it, couldn't torture herself with his flirtatious whims. He didn't care about her, and she didn't care about him. She wasn't into physical relationships, and this man was definitely not operating on an intellectual level. He was looking for a diversion on this voyage, and when the adventure was over he would discard her and find a new toy elsewhere.

She tried working off her tension by slapping some sandwiches together. She made a mockery of it, chopping off crusts, cutting the bread into weird shapes and sizes. The diversion helped some, but not enough to eliminate the turmoil Sam had managed to create.

Mack decided to treat herself to another brandy. The galley was well stocked with food and coffee and liquor—thanks to her foresight and her expense account. She unscrewed one of the miniature bottles and alternated between drinking and sandwich-making. It wasn't long before she felt warm and mellow from her head to her toes.

McPhee's arrogant behavior was probably normal for him. She shouldn't personalize it. He'd simply caught her off guard. She had no intention of involving herself with him, and she would tell him so as soon as she finished wrapping the sandwiches. As an afterthought, she stuffed two more of the little bottles of brandy in her pockets. Then she headed topside. Cold sea air might clear her head and bring some much-needed order to her thoughts.

On deck, Sam was soaking up what was left of the sunset. The ominous black clouds hanging in the northwest drew Mack's attention. She steadied herself and sucked in a breath of salt air and exhaled it with satisfaction. She'd taken time to run a brush through her loose hair.

"Sandwiches are ready," she said smoothly, grabbing hold of the wheel for balance.

As Sam bore down on her, she prayed her instincts for self-preservation would not drift away on the wind. Even in the evening light, she could see enough of him to be excited. She wondered if he planned to indulge in his pirate's mischief again. This time she would be ready.

He bent his head, his lips nearly touching hers, and Mack almost succumbed, almost fell into his familiar, warm embrace. But it was Sam who pulled back this time.

"Ah, cold cuts," he murmured. "They're right up there next to a hot bath."

Sam grinned, his teeth a flash of white in the moonlight, and braced himself against the wheel. White crests foamed beneath the boat's hull as the *Phoenix* sailed the black waters of Chesapeake Bay. The salty sea breeze had a sensuous effect on Mack, curling around her, caressing her, licking at her.

"Brandy?" she asked, waving the little bottle at him.

Sam studied it. Mack was hoping a drink would put him in the right frame of mind to hear what she was about to tell him.

"A peace offering?" he asked.

"Liquor's not a problem for you, is it?" she asked, deflecting his question.

"You want proof of character?" he said, his eyes glinting dangerously. "Give me the bottle of brandy."

Maybe she had pressed too hard, pushed too far. Sam's eyes locked with hers as he tipped the bottle to his lips, where he held it until he had drained the last drop from the little container. Mack suddenly had an unsettling feeling in the pit of her stomach.

"Do you always drink like this?" she asked, the bored tone back in her voice.

"Not always," he said, passing the empty bottle back to her. "But good brandy is more than drinking. It's almost an artistic experience."

She was momentarily ashamed of herself for judging him prematurely.

"Is there anything else you want proof of? Anything at all?"

Mack realized she'd been wrong about Sam; he was one of the lesser of her worries. Her own weakness for the arrogant man was her biggest concern. "No, you seem reasonably civilized," she said.

"I'll be howling at the moon before you know it." He reached out a hand and pulled her next to him. "You've been warned, lady."

She was prepared for his advance, and quickly slipped out of his grip, but not before his body brushed hers, leaving a tingling sensation in its wake. "Not this time, McPhee," she said. "I'm not interested."

"No?"

"No. And no means no."

"I've been known to become unpredictable," he murmured.

"Aggressive men are so boring," she said, hoping her voice didn't reveal the unsteady feeling inside her. "Predictability is never entertaining, wouldn't you agree?"

"Depends on the company," he said, his voice a husky, sensual growl.

He moved his hand to the front of her neck and caressed the sensitive skin there. Mack froze, expecting to feel one of his large hands graze her breast.

"Have a sandwich, McPhee," Mack said, in a throaty, dismissive tone.

Sam enthusiastically helped himself to one of the weird-shaped crustless wonders. Mack took a deep breath.

"Did you eat?" he asked, devouring half of the sandwich without paying particular attention to its shape or size.

"I don't happen to be hungry."

"It's your energy—you know, your blood sugar level. That's what's wrong. You don't eat enough to be cheerful. No wonder you're spaghetti-thin."

"Spaghetti-thin?"

His dark eyes surveyed her seductively, unabashedly, as though her reaction didn't matter in the least. "Well, everything that counts is in place...."

His attitude riled her, but Mack struggled to keep her ire under wraps. She tucked all the emotion she was feeling into some deep recess of her soul and just stood there, keeping her expression unreadable. She brought out the other brandy bottle and uncapped it.

"You've been hiding out all afternoon," Sam said, exercising all his charm.

Mack was standing close enough to him to breathe in the intoxicating scent of his skin. She reminded herself that she had absolutely nothing in common with this man. He moved way too fast for her. He was on intimate terms with adventure. He believed in living for today—no worries, no responsibilities, no cares. She'd been tempted by the excitement in his arms, but what she really wanted was security. What would a time-traveling pirate know about that?

"I've missed you," he persisted.

"I prefer being alone."

"That's exactly how I feel," he murmured huskily. "I want to be alone, with you."

"You don't have a humble bone in your body, do you?" Mack said, glaring at him.

"Why do you insist on complicating this?" he asked in a lazy voice.

"I don't want to be involved with you, Mc-Phee."

"I've made you mad again, haven't I?"

Mack just shrugged her shoulders at him. Mad? That was a perpetual state for her when he was close by. For a moment she lost herself to the soothing effect of the gently rocking boat and the damp sea breeze. Then, suddenly, the bow of the boat lurched forward.

Too startled to react, she stumbled into Sam's arms. He pressed her tightly against him and lowered his head until his lips were almost touching hers.

"Say it," he urged, his face so close that his warm breath was caressing her lips.

"S-say what?" she asked, an edginess to her voice.

"That you want me."

"Don't count on it!" Mack struggled to free herself. "I wouldn't want you if we were stranded together for eternity." She couldn't allow this— couldn't torture herself this way.

"But you do. You want me." He breathed the words into her ear. "Don't you? Just say it."

Mack's defenses were crumbling under the powerful strength of his muscled arms. Yes, dammit she wanted him...wanted to reach out and feel him . . . wanted him more than she wanted her next breath. . . .

Sam covered her mouth with his, thrusting his tongue deeper and deeper. Mack heard a groan of pleasure erupting from one of them, although which one, she wasn't certain. The brandy had freed her of any inhibitions, and she gave in to him with no second thoughts.

"Yes . . . I want you."

She clung tightly to him, blood pounding in her head as she pressed her mouth to his. Their tongues darted performing a ritualistic mating dance. She felt his touch everywhere, felt his hands kneading her breasts, felt his thumbs rubbing her nipples to erection. The flame between her legs blazed demandingly to life. Her urgency destroyed the last of her inhibitions as she felt herself coming alive against his arousal. The fantasy was back, and she was inside it, floating away on a cloud with her pirate, feeling no guilt, no shame—

"My God!" she suddenly cried out. "What are you doing? Put me down!"

Sam nearly dropped her, and Mack stumbled to regain her balance.

"Know what I like most about you?" he said hoarsely, in between ragged breaths. "A man always knows where he stands with you."

Mack's whole world was spinning out of control. Half of her regretted pushing him away, and the other half regretted urging him on.

Had she gone crazy? Kissing a homeless man, alone in the middle of the ocean? She felt thoroughly ungrounded, uprooted, as if her world had been strangely—irreversibly—altered.

# Chapter Six

Mack wondered if she'd lost her mind. It wasn't like her to be daring. And it wasn't like her to jump into the arms of a handsome pirate just because she'd been dreaming about an adventure like this one all her life. Sam McPhee had caught her unprepared. He'd entered her fantasy, but she couldn't allow him to enter her heart.

The noises of the gathering storm drifted into the cabin, which now rocked with a more pronounced motion. Mack flopped onto her bunk, buried her face in the pillow and punched out her frustrations on it. Her frustration wasn't because of what had nearly happened with Sam, but because of what *hadn't* happened. Sam's sheer physical strength had frazzled her nerves, and intensified her need for him. The man was driving her crazy. With all the resolve she could muster, she vowed to put a stop to this craziness with Sam McPhee. No more!

She froze when she heard her cellular phone ringing.

"What the hell is that?" Sam said, suddenly appearing in the small cabin.

Mack's heart leapt at the sight of him, and so did her new resolve—right out the porthole. She could explain the phone, but he would want to know who was calling. *Why not just come clean and tell him who her client was and what he intended to do with Sam's pristine island?* Mack's heart was pounding. The phone rang and rang. And Sam's determined expression demanded answers.

"My cellular phone," Mack replied. He deserved more of an explanation, but where would she find the words? Her secretive ways were catching up with her, and they were going to come between her and Sam, and there wasn't a damn thing she could do about it.

"You brought a phone?"

"I thought it would be a good idea."

She knew enough about Sam to understand that he wouldn't stand for anything less than the truth. A U.S. senator wanted his island. But if she identified her client, the plans for the dump site would come out, and then Sam would learn who her father was.

Sam looked silently down at her, piercing her with those raven-black eyes. "Aren't you going to answer it?"

The ringing persisted . . . five, six, seven times.

"Who's tending the boat?" Mack asked.

"We're anchored until I can radio the coast guard for another weather report," he said. "Now answer it!"

Mack rummaged with both hands through her duffel to locate the phone, and then pressed it to her ear.

"Hello?" she said.

"This is your answering service," announced an assertive voice laced with static. Mack had left instructions for the service to hold all her messages, so she knew this was going to be important. "A Ms. Gilley from Anderson and Associates insisted I get this message to you."

Mack whispered to Sam that her answering service was on the line, but the information didn't seem to affect him one way or the other. Apparently he didn't mean to give her any privacy.

"I'll take the message," Mack said, feeling very nervous. "But speak slowly. Your voice is cutting out."

She checked Sam's face for a reaction, but found none.

"Please hold," the voice said, without acknowledging Mack's request.

"No, wait—" Mack said.

Sam was devouring her with his intense gaze. Mack sensed rather than saw the change in him.

She recognized that look in his eyes, the same one she'd seen in them the first time they'd met. Even then it had had a profound effect on her, but now it reached all the way inside her heart and wouldn't let go.

Static filled the void; Mack suspected she was in for a lengthy wait, but then another voice exploded over the wire, monotone and impersonal.

"Just a moment, please," said the voice. "A Ms. Gilley's on the other line. I'll connect you."

"No!" Mack said, too late.

She was tempted to hang up, but she held on. Curiosity was only part of it. A small part. This was about fear. Fear of the unknown. Fear of exposure.

"Ms. Ford?" asked the impersonal voice of the senator's right-hand woman at his law firm.

"I'm here." Mack covered the phone receiver with her palm, and whispered to Sam that the caller was no one important.

"I don't give a damn if George Washington is on the other end," he answered tartly.

She held up a finger to indicate that she would be off the phone in just a minute.

"The senator has moved up the deadline," Ms. Gilley was saying. "You have two weeks to locate the man and secure this acquisition."

"Wait a minute," Mack argued. "You're changing the rules in the middle of the game."

"If you intend to further your career, you'll have a report on my desk within the next twenty-four hours. Is that clear?"

"That's always been clear." Mack muttered an oath as she tucked the telephone back in her bag.

"Your *client?*" Sam asked.

"My cellular phone is on your boat. That doesn't give you license to interrogate me about my calls."

"I got the impression that phone call was about me."

"That's because you like to think of yourself as always being center stage."

"Indulge my curiosity and tell me why my island is so important to your boss."

*So what's it going to be, MacKenzie?* Why couldn't she just tell him the truth? Sam crossed his arms and leaned against the door frame. He was all the more appealing—and daunting—in that sensuous stance, which accentuated the tautness of his lean body.

"What is this, McPhee—an inquisition?"

He hesitated, his eyes narrowing slightly. "You won't give an inch, will you?" he said, taking a deep, calming breath.

"I won't be compromised," she said, defending herself. "If that's a punishable crime, lead me to the gangplank."

"That's your problem, lady. You need to loosen up, both professionally *and* in your private life. We both know you want to live a little, and sooner or later I'm going to show you how. That's what's got you scared to death.''

"No, McPhee. Here's how it's going to be. If you want to get me into your bed, you'll have to arouse my curiosity first. I'm not afraid of you, I'm bored with you.''

"I'd forgotten that you're a thrill-seeker. Well, I'm not against old-fashioned foreplay to excite a lady,'' he murmured, so close to her that she felt his breath.

She shivered as she fought off the urgent desire that began at her core and moved upward so fast that the powerful sensation grabbed at her breath. Sam was dangerously charming.

But Mack had learned early on that men weren't to be trusted. And she despised everything Sam's vagrancy stood for. She'd been shouldering responsibilities since she turned twelve, but he had taken a back door to run away from life. That character flaw was one she refused to overlook.

"When I become excited, you'll know what I want because I'll tell you,'' she said.

"And my ear will be resting against your lips so that I don't miss a single word of it.''

Mack wasn't certain when he had lifted his hand, but he stroked her cheek now with his fingers. She was mesmerized into submission by the tingling sensation his touch left in its wake.

"Stop it," she said. "This isn't a game we're playing." Both of his hands gripped her now at her shoulders. "Let me go!"

"Then brace yourself," he cautioned. "We're in for a rough ride."

Suddenly Mack was all too aware of the turbulent rising and falling of the water, and she wondered if she was feeling the effects of the brandy. The cabin had turned into a giant rocking chair.

"Do you know how to use a two-way radio?" Sam asked.

"No, but it can't be too difficult."

"I'll show you," he said, urgently closing the distance to the little desk across from the galley area, and Mack followed. He lifted the mike and showed it to her. "See this button?"

"Yes."

"Depress it when you're talking. Release it when you want to hear the voice on the other end."

"I can manage that," she said.

Much to her surprise, her knees buckled underneath her, but only for a moment. When he tried to steady her, she pushed his arms away. She couldn't risk having his arms around her again. By now the boat was heaving up and down with predictable consistency, and she managed to balance herself without his help.

"Hold on," Sam said, pulling up a chair for her.

"I can do this myself."

"Do as I say," he replied.

Sam's words, which left no room for argument, startled Mack. No longer dazed, she realized the extent of his concern.

"What should I do?" she asked.

"Radio the coast guard in Norfolk. Their call numbers are written down here on this card." He pointed to a piece of paper on the desk top. "Give them our location—we're traveling east, north of Norfolk into the Atlantic. Get a weather report." He paused. "Can you do that?"

"I can handle it."

"Good," he said, in a deceptively tranquil voice. "You might be in for the thrill of your life." He started up the stairs, then turned back. "You won't be afraid?"

"You'd like that, wouldn't you? Having me vulnerable and at your mercy?

"I never take a lady against her will." That familiar pirate's grin spread sensuously across his lips. "*Are* you a lady, MacKenzie?"

Mack's hands were trembling as she held the mike. Her blasé attitude was an elaborate facade to cover up the pangs of desire shooting through her.

"That didn't seem to matter before. But right now, shouldn't you be concentrating on the storm you've got on your hands instead of making me your next victim?"

But as Sam returned topside, Mack didn't feel like a potential victim. She felt excited, aroused, and curiously warm inside....

SAM'S INTENSE ATTRACTION to Mack had thrown an unexpected wrench into the matter of getting to the bottom of her hidden agenda. Queeny's island wasn't a random choice for purchase, a piece of investment property an eager real estate agent recommended to a buyer with money to burn. Mack had the answers, but he was beginning to doubt whether her stanch refusal to divulge them could be cracked.

Sam didn't like to feel manipulated, but every time he got close to Mack, the experience left him weak and wanting more. He'd never been drawn so strongly to a woman. Now he had to admit to himself that his plan to seduce Mack into talking had simply been an excuse to do something he'd wanted to do from the first moment he saw her.

Admitting that simple truth explained a great deal more, like why he was on this cruise to Fantasy Island, on a small craft, in a storm, with one body to dispose of, and another body very much alive and driving him crazy.

The angry ocean bared its teeth as giant waves broke over the bow of the boat. It only took a second for Sam to realize that the storm had changed direction, intensifying as it prepared to chase the

*Phoenix* into the Atlantic. Lightning illuminated the sky, allowing him to assess his craft and the area around it. With no port nearby, the only choice was to try to outrun the storm.

The combination of salt spray and wind blowing through his lightweight clothing chilled him to the bone. He decided to hold off pulling up anchor until he'd checked with Mack about the weather report. Sam tucked his arms under his armpits and made his way downstairs to the cabin.

How could he have put Mack's life at risk like this? He couldn't imagine a future without her in it, which was crazy, considering how long they'd known each other. He hadn't even made love to her.... He had nothing to offer Mack right now in the way of a stable life, unless he was willing to slip back into a three-piece suit—but that possibility was crazy, too.

"Sam!"

Mack's voice sliced through the night like a knife.

"I told you to stay below," he growled. "Don't come any closer—you'll be swept overboard."

Breakers were rising from all directions, and the *Phoenix* slammed sideways into a giant one that sprayed water down onto them.

"What about you?"

"I can take care of myself," he muttered, feeling way too much concern for Mack. "Are you all right?" he called out to her.

"Soaked," she said, "but okay."

She'd changed into a white T-shirt and Levi's, which were clinging to her shivering body in a seductive way that nearly drove Sam crazy. In the clouded moonlight he could glimpse the outline of her nipples, which were protruding against the wet fabric of her top. Sam felt a tightening in his loins.

"Go below and get out of those wet clothes."

"But what about—?"

"I said go below!"

He hadn't intended to sound so gruff. Part of him wanted to carry her below, strip her naked, and kiss every inch of her luscious body until it was dry and she was begging for more. Water sprayed them again, and awareness flooded back through him.

Mack vanished down the hatch, to his great relief. He needed a good stiff drink to get him through this. Not the storm. The knowledge that Mack was below, making herself naked.

"WHAT ARE YOU DOING down here?" Mack said, glimpsing Sam as he hauled his body through the hatch right behind her.

"What did you find out?" he asked, moving within a few inches of her.

Mack's rain-soaked clothes allowed a thorough view of the body pressing against them. For a moment, Sam just stood there looking at her, measuring her, and she didn't like it. She could feel the heat in her cheeks beneath his appraising stare.

"Don't look at me that way."

Mack's resistance was wearing thin. The thought of Sam's strong arms around her was reassuring at the moment, but she willed it out of her head. She wished he would just go away.

"Are you going to tell me about the weather report, or do I have to radio for it myself?"

"The storm is gathering strength," she said. "But it's moving to the south, over West Virginia, and should miss us altogether if we're moving easterly."

"Come here," he said.

"No."

He stepped forward, slipping his arms around her, trapping her inside their warmth. He touched her neck, his fingertips cool and surprisingly smooth.

"What are you doing?" she demanded.

His busy hands seemed to be all over her, heightening her awareness and her anger.

"Get your hands off of me, McPhee."

"Will you hold still?" His breath was warm and sweet on her neck, where he was tracing her hairline. His touch was becoming more enthusiastic.

"Let go of me," she said, with a gallant attempt at sounding indifferent. "I know what you're doing. That's what makes you tedious—you're so predictable."

"I'm trying to put a life jacket around you," he said with a purely mischievous expression. "What did *you* have in mind?"

"I'd rather take my chances in the water," she said, certain all rational judgment had deserted her.

He backed away and tossed an orange life jacket at her. She caught it, but promptly discarded it.

"Since you can manage without me," Sam said, "I'd better see to the boat."

"Good!" she said.

"You like me," he murmured. "You like me a lot. That's what bothers you about me, isn't it?"

"I find you completely disgusting, McPhee. I despise arrogance in a man, and you are colossally vain."

"I like you, too," he said, his voice low, beguiling.

Mack stepped toward him angrily. She wanted to get her hands on him—for a multitude of reasons.

"Having a change of heart?" Sam asked, stopping her with one hand.

"Never!"

"I agree. The ambience is all wrong. I'll do you the honor once we reach land."

"The word *honor* is not in your vocabulary," she snapped.

"You're not going to let virginal timidity stand between us, are you? Especially when a deserted island is so near."

"Get out!" she said, in a tight, low voice. She sounded like a vicious dog about to go for the throat.

"Are you sure you don't want me to stay?"

For a moment she just stared at him. She couldn't believe she had to think about it. But at that instant, one part of her desired to be held and touched. But the other part of her wanted to pound the arrogance out of him.

"You've got a problem," she said, her nerves stretched to the breaking point.

Dark, curly hair fell onto his forehead. His beard almost covered the rest of his face, making it impossible to read his expression.

"Right," he said, lowering his face until his lips, warm and soft, brushed hers.

It was a gentle kiss, but it was enough to rekindle the fluttering sensation at her core. All the fight Mack had felt turned into burning passion. It seemed like the most natural thing in the world for him to take her right here, right now.

She kissed him back fiercely, clinging to him, blood pounding her brain as she pressed her mouth against his. She could feel every hard inch of his body pushing against hers. His tongue was driving, exploring, performing a ritualistic dance inside her mouth. Although fully conscious, she was losing control.

"What are you doing?" she demanded when she felt him pulling up her soaked T-shirt. She covered his hand with hers, and was surprised when the movement actually stopped him.

"Taking what I want," he murmured.

"You've got a problem."

"One hell of a problem," he agreed.

That wasn't entirely true, Mack admitted to herself. She was beginning to think that *she* was the one with the problem, and it was Sam McPhee.

# Chapter Seven

It had been a long night.

Sam aimed the *Phoenix* into the breakers and watched as she split them cleanly. They fell back to the foaming sea where they collected themselves to rise and strike again. The same way Mack forced herself into his thoughts, completely against his will. He could turn away from the sea, close his eyes to it, look the other way. But Mack was a different matter altogether. She refused to be ignored.

He hadn't had a decent night's sleep since he'd met her. He was bone-tired. All night Mack had slipped in and out of his head, keeping him warm against the cold and keeping his adrenaline pumping. He had managed to stay one jump ahead of the bad weather, but it had given him a scare. Now he was within a few miles of the island—and safety.

With daylight came the realization that the worst of the storm was behind them. The water remained rough, but sunshine bathed him as it spread across the expanse of blue sky. Nevertheless, being an experienced sailor, he wasn't taking any false comfort from the partial sunshine.

He had been checking on Mack off and on all night. Now he wanted to touch her again, feel the weight of her hair on his fingers, trace the outline of her mouth. But a glance at the sea squelched the temptation. Reality hit full-force.

The choppy, rolling waves had increased in size until the Atlantic had taken on a disturbed appearance. Ignoring his need to rest, Sam maintained his vigil, except for a periodic trip to look in on Mack. Sailing a woman to a deserted island had to be at the top of the list of absurd things to do.

He strained to look through for the island as the boat knifed ahead. According to Mack's map, it was close at hand. Sam was placing all his hopes in that.

At the helm, he dutifully watched his compass and closely observed every motion of the craft. He had spotted a tiny speck on the horizon at first light. As the sun lifted higher into the sky, so did the barrier island, rising up out of the Atlantic to greet them. But his relief at sighting the monolithic crescent of land was short-lived. There was now the possibility that they might run out of fuel.

He had studied the map carefully, and knew that less than a mile of beach existed on the whole of the island. The leeward side was little more than a marshy wilderness. The barrier side was the only safe place to anchor. Everything depended upon the accuracy of his calculations. To drop anchor even a few feet north or south of the desired point might mire them in serious, if not fatal, difficulties.

But at the exact moment the little craft rounded the northeast point of the island, the wind and the sea combined forces to take control of the *Phoenix*. Sam struggled to master the wheel again, to point the bow into the waves, expecting to run out of fuel at any moment.

"Damn these breakers," he muttered.

He worked to maintain control of the *Phoenix* as it plunged through the rolling surf. With the help of a strong current, the boat slid forward. Suddenly, Sam realized that the sea had seized control of the craft—the wheel had broken loose. It was no longer attached to or controlling anything. The swell of the surf breaking on the shore looked absolutely terrifying as Sam absorbed the enormity of what had just happened.

They needed a miracle to survive this, in spite of the fact that they were almost within a stone's throw to land. The Atlantic was playing with them, and it wasn't through yet. The possibilities of disaster were endless. The thundering roll of the ocean could smash them to bits after it beached them.

He struggled to regain control of the free-spinning wheel. Unless he could keep the bow pointed into the breakers, the sea would consume them. But the wheel had been rendered useless, disabling the small craft in the face of disaster. He prayed they would beach before capsizing. Left at the mercy of the sea, there was no choice but to ride out what had become a collision course with doom.

Sam forced himself to abandon the disabled wheel and go below to see to Mack. Guilt paralyzed him. He could only stand by and watch as the craft surrendered itself to the foaming swells that were shattering themselves on the strand. The force of the breakers was so great that the boat could easily be shattered before tipping over. He felt fear spreading through his stomach—not for himself, but for Mack.

He took a deep breath and imposed an iron control on himself. Nothing was going to happen to Mack. Not as long as he was still breathing.

Halfway down the cabin stairs, something with claws went flying over him. Lucky Pierre was making a hasty exit. When Sam looked into the cabin, he saw why. The ocean was swamping the boat.

"Don't be alarmed" was all he could think of to say to Mack, who was in her bunk, cramming things into her duffel bag.

"Do I look alarmed?" Mack asked, stepping out of the bunk and into the rising water. At that moment the boat tipped, and Queeny's box slammed into her, forcing her to grab on to it for support.

"Are you all right?" Sam asked. Fear knotted inside him. Just the thought of anything happening to Mack was enough to tear at his insides.

"I think so," she muttered, hastily lifting the lid of the box.

"Don't do that," Sam said in a harsh, raw voice.

"I'm just getting a life jacket."

"I have one for you!"

She didn't respond, except for the soft gasp that escaped her lips. Mack dropped the lid shut, and then stood there, looking amazed and very shaken. Shock siphoned the blood from her face.

"There's a *body* inside this box," she said, hardly able to lift her voice above a whisper.

Her huge blue eyes were full of unquenchable fear. Sam moved swiftly through the water to reach her, at the same time making a quick, involuntary appraisal of her body, which was now draped in a soaking-wet T-shirt and jeans. In one movement he closed the distance between them and gathered her into his arms. Too stunned to resist, Mack stood in his embrace.

"I can explain," he said in a low, composed voice, as if the answer were simple.

Twisting in his arms and arching her body, Mack sought to free herself from his hold. "Who's in that box?" she asked frantically.

Sam felt momentary panic. "Queeny," he murmured.

His large hand held her chin gently. His attitude became more serious. This wasn't the way he'd wanted the truth to come out about Queeny, but honesty was the most important thing here. It was the cornerstone of a relationship—which was a silly consideration, since there *wasn't* a relationship here. And never would be, since Mack would never be able to trust him again.

"*Queeny* has been traveling with us?" Mack asked, staring up at him with amazement in her eyes.

"Yes," he said, feeling enormous relief at no longer having to keep the secret.

She drew in her breath, as if afraid to hear what was to come next. "Sam...what's going on here?"

"Call it granting a dying woman's last wish. I didn't have the money to bury her and the mortuary was going to turn her remains over to the county. She would have ended up in a pauper's grave."

The look in Mack's eyes told him everything he wanted to know, and his heart melted. Tears of compassion fell down her cheeks, and she brushed them away. She didn't say it, but he knew she understood what this terrible confession was costing him.

"Don't cry," he said soothingly. "I didn't want to make you unhappy, I only wanted you to understand."

"I *don't* understand you, dammit," she whispered, her lips quivering.

He gathered her into his arms again and this time she sank into his cushioning embrace. Her soft curves molded to the contours of his body. Sam knew his desire had nothing to do with reason. Her nearness was simply overwhelming. He glanced uneasily over her shoulder at the rising water. The sound of more water gushing down through the hatch nearly brought his heart to an abrupt halt. The craft heaved, and Sam realized they would have to act fast.

"You've got to get out those clothes," he said, his voice uncompromising and filled with determination.

"What—what for?" she asked, trying to pull away, but he stopped her by grabbing hold of her wrists.

"Just listen to me," he said, in a harsh, raw voice. He could sense her confusion. It was true, he wanted her badly enough to take her right now, while they were sinking. But right now they had more dire problems to face. "Your clothes will pull you under."

Mack stared at him. There wasn't time to convince her.

"I should have known better than to trust you," she said stiffly. "Not a chance, McPhee."

"Either you take them off or I'll take them off for you," he growled, growing tenser by the second. "I don't want you on my conscience."

It was bad enough having her on his mind night and day.

"We're really sinking?" A flicker of apprehension lit her face. "Oh, my God..."

Sam swept her up into his arms. Too shaken by the news to resist, she went willingly, and said nothing when he deposited her on the bunk.

"Unbutton your jeans," he said, in a tone that brooked no debate.

"I think I understand," she said, in an icy voice.

He pulled off her tennis shoes, tossed them aside, then he began tugging on the legs of her Levi's. "Understand what?"

"That one way or another you do take what you want. That you probably diverted all this water down here just to make me vulnerable to your out-of-control animal instincts."

"Is that what you think?"

She held up a dismissive hand. "Don't bother giving me excuses. I wouldn't believe you."

Sam finished pulling her jeans off her, then he dropped them in the rising water. "If—and that's a very big if—we make it to shore," he said flatly, "you can tell me you're sorry. Provided you don't die in the process."

"The T-shirt stays," she said flatly. "Tell you I'm *sorry?* You won't hear those words from me— ever."

His appreciative gaze traveled the distance between her bikini panties and her lacy bra, which he had no trouble seeing right through her thin cotton top. The glimpse caused his heart to hammer inside his chest.

"You're beautiful," he said, the words slipping out seductively, like a soft caress.

The murky water licked at her long, luscious legs. The sound of it was driving him crazy. For one insane second, he imagined his mouth pressed against her naked body, tracing every inch of it up to her perfect breasts. In spite of her stature, her beauty was fragile, her body delicate.

"And you're disgusting," she fired back.

"Cover up with this," he said roughly, moving away from her as every nerve and sensation in his body screamed for him to touch her.

He tossed a life jacket at her, and she caught it, a confused expression on her face. She slipped it on, and her breasts disappeared underneath the bulk of it. He shifted his gaze upward to meet her eyes, and was already shrugging out of his own wet jeans when he spoke again.

"Are you a good swimmer?"

"Good enough," she said indifferently.

Her wide-eyed, alert expression belied her casual tone of voice. She grabbed her duffel bag from the berth and slipped her arms through the straps, securing it to her shoulders.

"What are you doing with that?" Sam asked. "Do you want to be pulled under?"

"It goes with me," she said fiercely.

"Have you looked around, lady?" he snapped. "We're sinking."

"And whose fault is that?"

"Stay here while I check topside," Sam said flatly. "We'll ride her as close to shore as she'll take us."

"I'm going with you."

"You're staying put, unless you want to be swept overboard."

A foam-crested wave washed into the cabin just then, silencing them as it pounded down the hatch. Another huge roller came in behind it, fiercely and rapidly. Worse, the stern of the boat, suddenly struck by the same wave, rose high in the air, forcing the bow under. When he looked back, Mack had disappeared.

*"Mack!"*

The next moment, the boat was lifted up by a great billow and swept furiously around until its bow was pointed directly out to sea. She broached to and fro, and began to roll over. The force of the breaker was sweeping Sam down.

"Mack..."

Something hard cracked his head, followed by a dark silence.

SAM'S BREATH CAUGHT in his throat. Water surged into his mouth, his eyes. He was going to drown and he didn't known which way was up.

Disoriented, he pushed with muscle-wrenching strength against the hard surface beneath him. Almost instantly he popped out of the water, gasping for air and coughing out water. It took him a moment to get his bearings. He was inside the cabin of the *Phoenix,* his only means of life support a tiny air pocket. Horrified, he realized the sloop was partially submerged, its bow pointing skyward.

Was Mack okay? Had she drowned? Had she been swept overboard? He had to save her...he had to... At the moment, nothing else in the world mattered to him.

Instinctively he dived. It was pitch-black in the cabin, and he could only feel his way in the gloomy water. Out of breath, he surfaced again. He shook the water off his face and blinked repeatedly. The salt stung his eyes. When the boat shifted, more water surged in. Time was running out. He dived again and again. The craft could sink now at any moment, trapping him on the ocean floor, but he wasn't leaving without her. If he couldn't find Mack, there would be no survivors.

Although the darkness prevented him from seeing anything, he swam with his eyes open, the salt water setting them on fire. He thought his lungs would burst. And what about Mack? Could she still be alive? Guilt seized him. He blamed himself. He should have hung on to her.

He resurfaced to the shrinking pocket of air, sucked in another deep breath and then pushed himself down again into the black water. His hand came down on something so soft it could only be human. Mack! He had gloried briefly in the discovery, but now he had to get her to air. How much time had elapsed, Sam couldn't be sure, but hope surged inside him as she grabbed hold of Mack's life jacket.

He floated easily through the stairway, fiercely holding on to Mack as he freed them from the sloop. But the dark water still held them, and a swift current slammed them downward. The sea had turned into an unrelenting beast, refusing to release them. Sam clung to Mack with both arms, using his legs to propel them away from the strong undertow. Then, without warning, the beast suddenly shoved him away from Mack—up, up through silence, faster and faster toward light, toward a voice...

He surfaced quickly, gasping and sucking at the air. A voice screamed. It was Mack's voice, calling for him. Without warning, the current slammed him under again. He'd found her only to lose her again.

He felt his lungs exploding as the force of the water pushed him along, until he finally came to rest. He remained utterly still—afraid the ocean would find him again, which it did, a breaker crashing down on him. But just as quickly it receded out to sea.

He opened his mouth to speak, but nothing came out. His ears rang. Coarse sand coated his flesh. He tried to focus his vision, but everything was blurred. When finally he could see, it stunned him to realize that the stern of the boat had been shot into the ocean floor like a bullet. Grimacing, Sam watched the *Phoenix* give way to the ocean—as though the entire mass of water had suddenly taken it into its mind to heave itself westward.

Hot pain shot through his head. His hands flew to his temples, pressing against them as if to neutralize the hurting somehow. Sam continued his attempt to ward off the pain, even as he was forced to submit to the blackness underneath another pounding breaker.

When it was finally through with him, he crawled for his life, crawled until he could feel dry sand underneath him. He collapsed only long enough to catch his breath. Another swollen wave surged and pounded the beach, crashing down on top of something Sam had spotted.

"Mack?" Sam uttered her name so faintly, he barely heard it himself. "Mack!" Now he flew along toward her. His heart began hammering when he realized he couldn't reach her before the next breaker came crashing down. He watched in horror as it hit Mack, full-force, burying her.

"DON'T YOU DIE on me now."

Mack heard Sam's voice somewhere in the blackness that enveloped her. She could smell wet sand, could taste it on her lips. Oh, God... She had nearly died. A terrified sob escaped her. Instantly she felt the warmth of Sam's arms on her, so bracing, so comforting, as he whispered reassurances.

Slowly she forced her eyes open.

"You're alive," she mumbled to Sam. Another foamy wave slapped at the beach.

"I am now," he muttered against her mouth. She felt his warm, confident hands on her body. "There's a laceration on your shoulder, but it doesn't look too serious."

She tried to smile her relief as he unfastened her life jacket. She felt no sense of shame, nor bruising of her pride, at the fact that she lay before him in her T-shirt and panties. He swept her, weightless, into his powerful arms, and for a moment just stood there, cradling her next to him, rocking her gently back and forth.

"I thought I'd lost you," he murmured.

"I never thought I would be saying this, but I'm sorry," she whispered, slipping her arms around his neck and resting her head on his shoulder. Then a thought occurred to her, and she pulled her head back to look at him.

"Lucky Pierre, and . . . Queeny?"

"Gone."

"I'm sorry, Sam," she said in a husky voice.

With deft movements, he carried her out of reach of the breakers and across the dunes, and stood her up under a thick, curling pine tree.

"Are you all right?" he asked, in a voice deep enough and sensual enough to send arrows of awareness through her.

"I think so . . . but I lost my glasses."

"You won't need them," he said, flashing his pirate's grin for the first time since they'd escaped the wreckage. "I'm the only man on the island."

"That's what I'm worried about."

She lifted her head to meet his gaze, and her body tingled with anticipation. He raised his hand to her cheek, and the touch was almost unbearable in its tenderness. She was suddenly conscious of where his warm flesh touched hers, where his breath fanned her face. He wrapped his arms around her, and his hands explored the hollows of her back.

Unable to think beyond the moment, Mack let herself be locked in his embrace. She clung tightly to him as she met his lips with her own. An ache within her grew more pronounced. She wanted him every bit as much as he wanted her.

THEY TORE AT each other with an urgency that refused to be denied. With his lips and hands, Sam explored every curve and recess of her body. He deepened his kiss, wanting all of her, and she yielded her mouth to his lips. Soon he felt her heartbeat quickening against his chest. He responded by pulling her down with him onto the sand and sliding a leg between hers.

Sam pressed her to him, his mouth seeking hers. He couldn't help himself—he wanted her. His thoughts raced dangerously.... He and Mack were shipwrecked, without food or water or shelter, and all he could think about was making untamed passionate love. Their mouths met, sweet and warm as they joined, and his need for her intensified. His hands moved underneath her T-shirt, where they turned urgent and demanding.

When she drew away, he gasped, too close to the edge to turn back. Mack stood up and stretched her arms high overhead to rid herself of her shirt. Her hands reached up to unfasten her bra, which she watched fall to the ground. All that remained was her panties, and she shimmied out of those, too. Then she stared down wordlessly at Sam.

He swept his gaze over her body. She was more beautiful than he'd even imagined. Streaks of sunlight through the tree limbs illuminated the dampness on her skin, the erectness of her nipples. Her breathing was shallow and rapid, and her breasts rose and fell with every breath. There had been a change in her, Sam thought. She was bolder, brasher, and she was holding back nothing as she eased down beside him.

His need erupted into a hot tide of passion that drove him to the very edge. He shrugged off his shorts and reached for her. His lips met hers in a crushing kiss. One hand moved down over the curves of her body, his exploring fingers tracing a path to the core of her. She was ready when he slid first one finger, then another, deep inside her, taunting, teasing, finally withdrawing to lift her to him.

A moan escaped his lips. He traced the lines of her nipples with his tongue, taking one into his mouth to suckle until she was writhing beneath him. He abandoned that nipple and took the other one, his tongue darting, teasing, until visible tremors moved through her body with escalating need. She was ready. Sam savored the sensation as he allowed her body to slide down his.

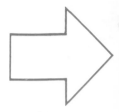

# NO COST! NO OBLIGATION TO BUY!
# NO PURCHASE NECESSARY!

## PLAY ''LUCKY 7''
## AND GET AS MANY AS FIVE FREE GIFTS . . .

# HOW TO PLAY:

1. With a coin, carefully scratch off the silver box at the right. This makes you eligible to receive two or more free books, and possibly another gift, depending on what is revealed beneath the scratch-off area.

2. Send back this card and you'll receive brand-new Harlequin American Romance® novels. These books have a cover price of $3.50 each, but they are yours to keep absolutely free.

3. There's no catch. You're under no obligation to buy anything. We charge nothing—ZERO—for your first shipment. And you don't have to make any minimum number of purchases—not even one!

4. The fact is thousands of readers enjoy receiving books by mail from the Harlequin Reader Service®. They like the convenience of home delivery. . . they like getting the best new novels months before they're available in stores . . . and they love our discount prices!

5. We hope that after receiving your free books you'll want to remain a subscriber. But the choice is yours—to continue or cancel, anytime at all! So why not take us up on our invitation, with no risk of any kind. You'll be glad you did!

**This lovely Victorian pewter-finish miniature is perfect for displaying a treasured photograph—and it's yours absolutely free—when you accept our no-risk offer.**

# PLAY "LUCKY 7"

**Just scratch off the silver box with a coin.
Then check below to see which gifts you get.**

**YES!** I have scratched off the silver box. Please send me all the gifts for which I qualify. I understand I am under no obligation to purchase any books, as explained on the back and on the opposite page.

154 CIH AKWQ
(U-H-AR-08/93)

NAME

ADDRESS _____ APT

CITY _____ STATE _____ ZIP

| 7 7 7 | WORTH FOUR FREE BOOKS PLUS A FREE VICTORIAN PICTURE FRAME |
| 🍒 🍒 🍒 | WORTH FOUR FREE BOOKS |
| ● ● ● | WORTH THREE FREE BOOKS |
| 🔔 🔔 🍒 | WORTH TWO FREE BOOKS |

But he held back until, after lowering her to the sand, he thrust himself inside her with one swift motion. The pleasure was pure and unbridled as their bodies moved in exquisite harmony. His impatience for release grew to explosive proportions.

Sam anchored her with his weight and allowed the frantic, writhing motion of her body to drive him to the edge again and again. Urgency took over, and he braced her rocking hips with his hands and drove himself into her until he felt her body stiffen. She cried out his name, and he felt their souls touching as he released.

He relaxed enough to roll over, pulling Mack with him, refusing to let go, staying inside her. His fingers traced the fine lines of her lithe body. Her breathing had slowed to an even pace, but now it was quickening, signaling that she was ready for him once more.

Wordlessly they made love again, extending and savoring the pleasure this time. Before, his passion had raged out of control, but this time he was setting the pace.

He held on until he felt her hips rising to meet his, until he felt her fingers digging into the small of his back, until her body arched and shuddered uncontrollably with pleasure. Then he let himself go inside her.

After the last spasm had rippled through his body, he quietly untangled himself and slipped off her, a hand brushing across her breast. He felt her exhale a long, shuddering sigh. He wanted to reach for her, pull her into his arms and comfort her. Above all, he wanted to assure her that everything was going to be all right. But he couldn't, not with any certainty.

Mack reached for her T-shirt and panties and dressed. Then she handed Sam his shorts.

She looked over at him with huge, luminous blue eyes. "I'm scared."

"It's okay to feel that way. It will help us to stay on our toes and find a way out of this mess."

"It won't take long, I hope," she said distantly.

"It shouldn't if we can locate your cellular phone. If it's still working, you can call whoever it was who sent you here, and have them come for you."

"We'll call the coast guard."

"Who sent you here, Mack?" He could feel her go cold and stiff next to him. But he was determined. "What difference does it make if I know now?"

"None, I suppose, but—"

Without preamble, a deep rumbling sounded, like the last breath pushing its way out of a giant. Sam's heart suspended its beating as he rose to view the *Phoenix*. The beached craft was still rumbling as it settled, its keel clearly visible, its stern pointing into the ocean floor, and its bow reaching for the sky as if in a last effort to save itself from certain doom. Its mast lay dutifully on its side, but the sail was still intact.

They made their way toward the disabled craft, walking at first, then running. They kept going even as a huge breaker crashed on the beach, licking at their feet with its white, foaming tongue. Finally the *Phoenix* rested directly in front of them. Sam didn't know what he would find. As far as he knew, Queeny had had her burial at sea, and Lucky Pierre was with his mistress.

"Don't get any closer," Sam cautioned her in a stern tone. "It's too dangerous. The craft could break apart under the next wave."

Mack blinked in acquiescence.

"Don't worry," he said, dredging up false optimism. "Everything will work out."

He felt like a heel. He wanted to make everything right, but he knew damn well he couldn't.

WHETHER her sigh was of pleasure or relief, Mack didn't know, but she collapsed back onto the sand to assess their situation. Not just the part about being stranded on a deserted island, but also the one about a tall, dark, mysterious pirate. There was no future for her with a homeless man. Nothing was making sense . . . except her body's craving for the strength and the warmth of his flesh.

Sam had climbed the mast and was hanging from a rope while he freed the sail. Even from this distance she could appreciate how rigid and strong his deeply tanned body was. Few working men had a body like his. He had no job, no permanent address, and yet he had a physique most women only dreamed about lying next to.

Mack pressed the heel of her hand to the skin between her eyes and took a deep breath of salt air, hoping it would clear her head. When the aching in her shoulder started up, she was almost grateful for the diversion. The skin there felt sticky and wet. When it began to throb, she wondered what she could do for it without a first aid kit.

A troop of brown pelicans spotted the blue sky, gracefully performing an unnamed ballet, dipping and falling with the air currents.

During the lull between waves, her attention was drawn to something in the sand. It lay midway between her and the *Phoenix,* and she darted ahead, dangerously close to the ship. She bit her lip to stifle a cry of delight. But she couldn't hold it back.

"Sam! Sam!" she called out. "Come down and see what I've found."

He had succeeded in freeing the sail, which he allowed to fall into the water. Then he shimmied down the rope, looking as wild as Tarzan in one of those old adventure movies that she had always loved watching. His queue had come loose, and for the first time she saw his long hair blowing freely around his face. No wonder she was going crazy. The man was irresistibly sexy. She held her breath when he jumped into the water, too.

"This ought to cheer you up," he said, dragging up the huge piece of canvas. "We'll have a place to sleep tonight." The wicked glint in his eyes said the rest.

*We?* She wanted to protest, but she already felt self-conscious enough standing there in her panties and T-shirt. And a real shelter was too tempting to turn down, even if the notion of sleeping with Sam McPhee was driving her mad. She intended to keep a respectable distance from his delectable body.

"Take a look at this." She was purring like a cat with the catch of the day.

"Your duffel bag?" he asked incredulously. "I can't believe it floated to shore. Anything in there that will fit me?"

*Not with that physique,* Mack was tempted to say. "No, but there's bottled water, peanut butter crackers, my cellular phone..." She broke into a smile in spite of herself. "Even a laptop computer." She felt very relieved that she'd bought special waterproofing plastic to cover her things.

"Just when I was beginning to like this place, the lady decides to call a cab." Sam bit thoughtfully at his lower lip. "Stick around and find out just how talented I am."

"How can you tease about this? Don't you have anyone waiting for you at home? Where *is* home for you?"

"What is this, twenty questions?" he said in a dismissive tone. "Better let me help you with that."

He took the duffel from her and, carrying the bag and dragging the sail, moved inland to the dunes.

"Let's have a look," he said.

"It's a good thing I didn't listen to you about leaving it behind," she said, regaining control of herself and forcing the excitement from her voice.

Mack set about opening the bag to dig inside for her cellular phone. She pulled out bottled water and peanut butter crackers first. Then came the technological wonder.

"Well?" Sam said. Mack could feel the intensity in his lowered voice.

She couldn't stop her hands from shaking as she unfolded the phone. When finally she'd opened it, pushed all the right buttons and held it next to her ear, she watched her disappointment register on Sam's face as she shook her head to indicate that it wasn't working.

"Let me try it," he said.

His large hand held hers gently as he accepted the phone, sending a shiver of awareness through her. Mack was determined to keep a comfortable distance from Sam. But exactly how she was going to do that, she didn't know.

"What's the point?" she said resignedly. "You can't expect to call for a cab when you're shipwrecked. You'll have to come up with another solution, McPhee—a more realistic one."

"I think I have," he mumbled, taking the phone apart. "All this little baby needs is to have her batteries charged."

"Don't play with me," she said defiantly. "This is serious. And at the moment we're without electricity."

"That's true enough, but if we had another battery, like—"

"The *Phoenix*," she finished for him, a new edge of excitement in her voice. The rush was shortlived. "But that battery is made of lead, and it probably weighs as much as you do."

"What are you so grumpy about?" he asked.

"What do you think? I was hoping to free myself of this sandbar—and you."

"You're the one who wanted to sail to a deserted island," he pointed out, standing to look around. "Looks like I'm the only man, too. So try to control yourself. You've been all over me ever since I hit the beach. You'll wear me out."

"Just get this straight, McPhee. I don't want to become involved with you." She wanted to make herself clear. "Forget whatever it was that happened between us, because it never happened."

He paused to look around. "Not a bad site for a convent."

"You're on the right track, McPhee."

"I'm not against celibacy," he said seductively, his extraordinary eyes gleaming, "but I don't think you're cut out for it."

His words sent currents of desire through her, and she realized the enormity of her body's appetite for him, whatever her head might say. She cursed her lack of willpower. If she'd had any delusions about what Sam was after, things were clearly in focus now.

"Shelter is our first priority," Sam said. "We need a windbreak, and those trees will serve the purpose."

"That's too far inland. We've got to think about being spotted. And look at that grass. Anything could be crawling around in it."

Live oaks littered the dunes. Some were huge and lush, with branches that had grown together overhead, creating a canopy of shade and a partial refuge from rain.

"We'll lose the windbreak if we stay on the beach," Sam objected. "And the sun beating down on the sand will burn us up during the day."

"No."

"Come on," he said, reaching with his hand to rub the back of his fingers across her cheek. "We'll make a lean-to with the sail on one of the dunes closer to the trees."

"No," she repeated flatly.

"No?"

"We need visibility. We'll stay on the beach."

"We'll burn up on the beach," he said, growing impatient. "Come on, or I'll tie you up in this sail and drag you."

One assessing gaze over his powerfully muscled body assured her that he could—and probably would—do just that. His damnable arrogance was driving her mad. At the same time, something in his manner soothed her.

"That was a stupid stunt, risking your life for that sail."

"You didn't have to worry about me. I'm a strong climber."

"It wasn't you I was worried about," she snapped.

"I like the way your eyes light with fire when you're mad," he said, in a low, husky tone. "Your biggest trouble, lady, is that you don't know how to loosen up. Things could be worse, you know."

"Don't you get it? We're not tourists here, we're victims."

"That's your problem," he murmured, in an even sexier tone. "Try to relax. It's something you need to do more of."

"You are crazy, aren't you?" Mack squeezed her eyes shut in disbelief. "Oh, God, I must be crazy, too, because I'm here with you."

"Crazy is subjective, you know," he said, standing way too far inside her comfort zone. She *had* to be insane to be entertaining the kinds of thoughts she was having about his body.

"I'd love to talk more with you about it, but we've got more pressing problems," Sam said. "Like where we're going to sleep tonight."

The two of them sleeping together....

Mack tucked the thought away, but it would return, she was certain of that.

## Chapter Eight

Mack moved with easy grace as the two of them set about fashioning a lean-to out of the canvas sail. She'd turned a T-shirt into a midriff-length sleeveless pullover that allowed Sam to admire her taut stomach. Her narrow hips tapered into long, straight legs. He couldn't forget the way they'd felt around him, and her breasts were also a constant, agonizing reminder of their powerful lovemaking. He could honestly say that he'd been to heaven and hell, all in the same day.

Sam estimated that the island was approximately twenty-five miles east of Virginia Beach. Maybe. But those few miles might as well be thousands. Unless they were in a shipping lane, it was unlikely they'd be discovered any time soon. Yet it was also possible that Mack knew more than she was telling.

"Why don't you level with me about this island?" he said, keeping his eyes on what he was doing with the sail. "You're only buying time, you know." He paused to assess her reaction. But Mack had the ability to absorb a direct hit and recover before he could discern her feelings. "I think you want to tell me," he said, attempting a bluff.

He'd admired the way Mack pitched in to gather rocks to secure the canvas to the dune. The shelter was turning out better than he'd expected. At least it would protect her fair skin from the hot sun.

"I'm not interested in what you think," she said, with a mischievous tone in her voice. "I should have left you in jail when I had you there."

"You couldn't have stood being separated from me. And I have to admit, my life hasn't been the same since I met you."

"Is that what you think?" she said, straining to control her rising indignation.

"I thought you weren't interested in what I think."

Mack flinched. "Don't count on anything, McPhee," she said coolly.

"You like that, don't you—keeping me guessing?"

"Excuse me?"

"Sooner or later you'll play your wild card—and when you do, it'll be winner-take-all."

"Wrong, McPhee," she said sweetly, closing the distance between them. "I've already played my wild card."

She was dangerously close, and Sam could feel the warmth of her body next to his. And, of course, he pulled her into his arms. She flailed her arms and legs in resistance, which nearly drove him mad with intense sensation.

"Now admit it," he said, his voice deep and husky. "You want me, too, don't you?"

He couldn't think clearly. All the blood seemed to have rushed from his head to his groin.

"Of course I do," she said innocently. "And I'm going to take good care of you, because you're my ticket out of here. Get it, McPhee? I need you to stay alive."

He'd never met a woman like Mack. Deceptively tempestuous, physically appealing, and smart as hell. He knew what she thought about him. But he also understood that what her body was telling him belied everything else. And from the flicker of wild abandon in her eyes, it was obvious that she knew it too.

"I've never felt more alive in my life," he said, his voice suddenly gentle.

"It—it's time we set some priorities here."

"There's just you and me and the magic that's waiting to happen." For a brief, heated moment, they locked gazes. "Nothing else makes much sense now, does it?"

Mack appeared at a loss for something to say. Why couldn't she just go on instinct and let this thing that was growing between them have its way? He knew damn well how she felt about him, and here they were, thrown together by fate on a deserted island. He found the idea exciting.

"Look, Sam," she began, in a tone that brooked no argument, "things are complicated enough. Can't we just get on with setting up camp? We've got survival to worry about. We can't just sit around waiting to be rescued...."

"Rescued?" he said, in a bored tone of voice. "I'm looking forward to an exotic vacation. Where's your sense of adventure?" He lowered his voice to a husky growl. "Do you know how badly I want you?"

Mack edged away from him, but not before she made the mistake of looking at him with eyes full of desire she didn't want him to see. "But if you want to hold out a while longer, what can it hurt? I'll still be here," he said, feeling amused again. He would still be here, all right.

"How can you minimize our situation?"

*Minimize it?* Hell, there was no way he was going to survive unless he figured out a way around her intoxicating spell. Sam glanced over at her, catching the glint of confusion in her eyes, and was pleased that he could throw her off balance.

"Why so tense?" he asked. This will all come to an end soon enough, and you'll find yourself back in that concrete jungle.

His hand was gentle when he reached up to touch her face again. She tried to pull away, but he stopped her by pulling her so close that their bodies were pressing against each other.

Still, she wriggled to free herself, prompting Sam to ask, "Do you have any idea how impressed I am with your enthusiasm?"

He braced himself for her reaction, thinking it might range from the tame to the exciting, but what he got was neither.

"Give it up, McPhee," she said in a monotone. "I've got you all figured out. You shroud yourself in mystery because it makes you appear larger-than-life. But my life's at stake here. We need shelter, food, water. I need your help—"

She grew silent and brooding. Sam knew he had to think of something quickly. He was so afraid she might suddenly start to break down. And it was way too soon for either of them to start giving up.

"There's a quick, simple way off this island." Instantly, he had her attention. But when she nailed him with those big blue eyes, he lost his train of thought for a brief moment. "We'll build a four-alarm fire," he said, pleased with his creativity.

"What are you talking about?" she said in a dismissive tone.

"I'm talking about ordinances limiting burning. We'll build a fire, and before you know it the Virginia beach patrol will be here with a water hose and an illegal-burning citation," he said, satisfied that he had, for the moment, distracted her thoughts from their precarious situation.

"We just want to get rescued. We don't want to go to jail. Are you suggesting that we break the law to get attention?"

"Something like that," he said, wanting to touch her, hold her, reassure her. For a brief, delicate moment, Sam realized just how vulnerable she really was. "Look here, you're bleeding," he said, keeping his voice casual.

"I am?"

He lifted a tattered flap of her T-shirt to assess the extent of the injury. The wind tugged at her clothing and her hair, revealing just how perfect her body was. She was mannequin-thin. At times he could even see her ribs. He attempted to focus his attention on her injury.

"You've got a nasty laceration," he said, "but you're in good hands."

Holding her startled glance for a moment, he tried to reassure her. "I won't leave your side for a minute."

"Sorry to disillusion you, but you've got me confused with someone who gives a damn."

"You look sexy when you get all hot and bothered and flushed."

"I am not flushed. I'm not—I mean, in case you hadn't noticed, the temperature's rising."

"Oh, I'd noticed."

"Then could you hurry up with this lean-to?" she asked, a tremor in her voice. "I could use the shade."

She was right about the humidity. And about finishing the shelter, too. Collecting sufficient wood might require what was left of the afternoon, and the evening, too. Apprehension tightened the knot in his stomach. He looked beyond the white sandy beach to the dark, shadowy green forest of loblolly pines and live oaks. A stiff wind pushed at them, and they resisted, displaying their unyielding strength.

A pounding breaker crashed on the beach, calling Sam's attention to the *Phoenix*. The craft, with its broken mast and torn and flapping sails, looked like a huge beached whale, belly-up and helpless. A sobering thought occurred to Sam. Everything in the world they needed for survival was inside that partially submerged boat—including the battery.

Even so, he was as determined as ever that they were going to survive this. He had Mack to think about now.

"WHAT HAPPENS NEXT?" Mack asked when at last the lean-to was secured in place with rocks and they had inventoried their meager supply of food and water. They'd even had enough canvas left over to cover their beds of sand. Crude as it was, the shelter looked inviting and safe.

"I don't know," Sam said honestly, "but at least we're alive."

Mack realized it wasn't easy for him to sound cheerful, particularly under the circumstances.

"That's all that matters—that and setting some priorities, like tending to our injuries, shelter, food and water." He looked at her. "Come on, Mack, are you with me on this? I can't do it all by myself."

"You're right, I suppose," she said, her voice little more than a whisper. "Things could be worse. I'm . . . I'm glad I'm not alone."

Knowing she had Sam by her side was enough to lift her spirits. Otherwise she could easily imagine giving in to the panic that was just around the corner. She caught sight of him out of the corner of her eye. He had a ruggedness and a vital power about him that had attracted her from the moment she first laid eyes on him. Now she was depending on his strength for survival. And that was what was spinning her thoughts out of control.

There was never any question as to how things were going to end up between them, not after he'd saved her life, not after she'd woken up in his arms on the beach. Trusting Sam was not the problem. Resisting his overwhelming magnetism was.

"What changed your mind?" he asked.

"I didn't have any other choice."

"Damned if that isn't what I love about you," he said, real humor in his deep voice.

It took a lot for her to admit she needed him. She was a determined woman who was used to doing things her own way. But for a while, anyway, Sam was going to be at her side. Mack not only had to survive the island, she had to survive aching for the fulfillment of his lovemaking, and her intensifying feelings for him.

MACK LAY so close to Sam that he could hear her breathing, slow and even, after sleep finally won out. Curled into a little ball, with the firelight radiating on her magnificent body, she appeared demure and vulnerable. He couldn't understand her self-consciousness. Any man would find MacKenzie Ford desirable. It puzzled him that she didn't seem to realize that. And it was driving him crazy.

He inhaled a deep breath of salt air. From the ocean, only a few hundred yards away, came the dull rumble of the crashing waves. He stirred the fire and stared at the glowing coals. His entire life had changed irreversibly when he made love to Mack.

Allowing himself to become vulnerable to another woman would be a major mistake. It was exactly what he didn't want. The fact that he was feeling as though he couldn't live without Mack frightened him. At the moment, he had nothing to offer her, nothing to give her, except himself. And he had already given her that when he rescued her—and then, thoughtlessly, gave himself over to passion and made love to her.

Mack stirred, looking more delicate than ever. Sam watched with satisfaction as she revived herself. She had been fueling herself all day on sheer adrenaline. And nerves. She stretched out her luscious body, blinking herself awake, her hair splayed across the canvas beneath her making her appeal devastating. Today she had demonstrated a strength and stamina completely at odds with the slenderness of her body.

"Cold?" he murmured.

Along with a fresh halter top, she had slipped on a clean pair of shorts she'd ferreted out of her duffel bag. He liked her better without anything covering her exquisite body, but there was still endless leg showing for him to admire. She tensed under his scrutiny.

"Comfortable," she said in a husky voice.

She looked at him with the wide-eyed innocence of a child, and he felt ashamed of the thoughts that were racing through his mind. She viewed him as a homeless indigent. Only the truth could fix that, and he didn't care to declare it just yet.

"The breeze turns chilly after sundown," he said, anxious to share the canvas blankets he had fashioned out of the leftover sail.

He reached for them, thinking that sooner or later he would have to level with her. He wanted her badly enough to face his deceptions. He knew, too, that the truth always reared its head sooner or later—although in this case he hoped it would be later.

"I can take care of myself, McPhee," she said in an icy tone. "Why don't you do the same? We're not Tarzan and Jane."

"I see you're feeling better," he said flatly, tossing the blankets aside. "I'll be here. If you need anything from me, you'll have to ask." He meant it, and his tone said as much.

"You saved my life today, and you were rewarded for it. The debt's paid. Don't count on getting anything else from me."

"You'll change your mind," he said, turning to look at her. "You know you're crazy about me." He flashed his most seductive grin at her, amused at how fast he could raise her ire.

"I've always despised arrogance in a man, and you're no exception."

"It's what I do best."

"What you're best at is taking what you want."

Maybe he was teasing her too hard about her feelings for him. In truth, he was only doing it to distract her from their problems. But he hadn't missed the tremor beneath her skin when he pulled her next to him—a tremor that had nothing to do with fear. Maybe he was arrogant, but he couldn't help thinking what a paradise this place could be if this damn woman weren't so intent on fighting her attraction to him. It wasn't smugness Sam was feeling, it was wild, crazy desire.

"I think I'll go back to sleep," she said.

She was staring at him again with those huge, curious blue eyes of hers, and any trace of smugness he'd felt disappeared. He'd spaced their beds two feet apart to accommodate the width of the lean-to, but what he had actually done was create a torture chamber for himself. All night he would have to think about her delectable body lying within reach. How was he supposed to forget that they had been intimate? And how was he supposed to suppress the spark of excitement at the prospect of its happening again?

He wished he had a slug of whiskey to numb his senses. He admired Mack in the light of the nearly full moon. She had an angelic innocence about her, lying there bathed in moonlight. But he had made love to the other woman, the one hiding behind the controlled facade—the bold, sensuous, totally beguiling woman.

For one enchanted minute, he forgot everything and indulged in the moment, thinking how the moonglow transformed the evening into something magical. The sea had a sprinkling of moonbeams dancing on it.

Eyes still closed, Mack suddenly announced, "I'm a light sleeper." Her silken words spilled into the quiet that stretched between them. "So keep your distance, McPhee."

"There's hardly any distance to worry about," he said, in a voice so low he wasn't certain it reached her. "The night will take care of itself."

"I'm warning you . . ." she cautioned.

"Go to sleep," he said roughly.

Sam watched her closely while he moved to stir the coals back to life. He pushed and shaped a ring of sand around their campsite, topping the ridge with hot coals to discourage anything undesirable from crawling in to share the space with them. Their newfound world looked magical as he watched Mack drift off to sleep.

It had been a long day. As he soaked up the heat from the fire, he realized it was time to make a decision. Their survival depended upon their making the right one. The *Phoenix* had the two things they needed most in the world right now: bottled water and a battery. He might be able to recharge Mack's cellular telephone, which could put them in touch with civilization. He told himself he should be happy, excited, but he wasn't. How was it that he felt as if coming to the island were the best idea he could ever have come up with?

Postponing the dive posed a serious risk. If the *Phoenix* dislodged and floated out to sea on the strength of the receding tide, they would probably face certain doom. Yet diving during high tide could cost him his life, and he could hardly risk that, when Mack's life depended upon his staying alive.

But within two days they would be out of water, which would put a whole new spin on their situation. Barrier islands seldom had natural water sources.

Sam made the decision to dive.

## Chapter Nine

When Mack awoke, she was alone, wrapped snugly in a canvas blanket. The first thing she remembered was Sam making magnificent love to her. It was just as well that he was gone. She needed the time out to draw her line of defense. She had worked too hard to build a solid life to let the likes of Sam McPhee take her world by storm. She was disciplined and capable of coping with the strongest craving she had ever felt for another human being.

The hands on her watch read eight o'clock. It couldn't be that late! But the position of the sun confirmed it.

She scanned the beach and spotted Sam bending over something she couldn't make out. She thought it looked like the box that... But that was ridiculous.

"Okay," she said, drawing a deep breath that she hoped would fill her with resolve. "Let's go down and have a look."

Trying to hurry barefoot across the dunes wasn't easy, especially when the sand was hot from the bright sun. She told herself that even if it was *the box,* there was nothing frightening about a corpse. Her gaze wandered toward the object again, and she stared, her breath catching in her throat. Sam had the lid open.

Queeny was back.

She had assumed the unusual freight would be on its way to Tahiti by now, along with Lucky Pierre. Poor kitty. A pang of guilt stabbed at her conscience over the cat's fate.

"Sam?" she said softly, close enough now to touch him. "Oh.... God...I thought it was a dream."

"It's a hell of a lot more than a dream." His voice, though deep, was crisp and clear.

"We must be on a mission from God," she said. How were they going to bury a body without any tools?

"Could be," Sam said with resignation. "Queeny was surely one of His angels."

"Everything's going to work out," Mack said. "I think this is an omen."

"A good one, I hope," he said, in a tone that held a degree of warmth and concern.

The two of them dragged the box across the dunes to a fitting burial site. After scanning the area for a suitable spot, Sam finally decided on a place where the dunes met the trees.

"If you don't think you're up to this," he said, intensity in his lowered voice, "I'll understand."

"I want to help," she protested. "I practically feel like I knew her."

"I was considering that knoll over there." Sam pointed to a rise about thirty yards away. "It won't be easy getting the box there, but the site is well beyond the high tide line."

She wondered how Sam was fueling himself. There was a restless energy about his movements. Her mind burned with the memory of his body thrashing against her own, and the ecstasy of being joined with him.

"Time out," she said, feeling as if her arms were going to break. "The sun's getting intense."

"The longer we stand around discussing it, the hotter it gets," he said flatly. "If you can't handle it, go back to camp."

"Are you saying you don't want my help?"

"No," he said, his tone suddenly docile. "I'm saying I think you've bitten off more than you can chew."

His grin was inappropriate, no matter how devilishly seductive.

"Fine, McPhee. Then do this alone."

She had just turned away and begun the walk back to camp when she felt his hand on her arm.

"Where do you think you're going?" he thundered.

"I'll go where I please," she said fiercely, tugging at his arm.

"I'm ... sorry," he said simply. "I need your help."

She shrugged out of his grip and calmly assumed her position again.

The box, which was wet, had taken quite a beating. Mack knew there was a good chance it could come apart if they put too much strain on the rope. But, in spite of everything, Sam's mood seemed suddenly buoyant.

Mack imposed an iron control on herself, feeling a strange, numbing comfort in the fact that Queeny was back. After all, if it hadn't been for her, she might never have met Sam, who, she couldn't deny, made her feel good.

"A shovel would come in handy right now," she suggested.

"There are enough tools on the *Phoenix* to build a house."

"And I was worried about the accommodations."

It was difficult to keep her gaze off his arms. The powerful muscles on them stood out as he pulled Queeny's box toward the interment site.

"This ought to do it," he said quietly when they'd reached the agreed-upon spot.

Sam spent most of the morning digging a hole, using his hands and a flat rock. But it was the sandy soil that allowed him to dig a proper grave. The ceremony was mercifully brief. Sam gave the closing words, and the tenderness in his expression moved Mack. She was beginning to realize that there was a lot more to this man than met the eye.

"Lord, take Queeny into your flock and keep her—"

"Look!" Mack interrupted, pointing overhead. "I can't believe it! I think it's a bald eagle."

"Damned if it isn't."

The magnificent creature soared on the breeze, its powerful wings casting an impressive shadow below.

"Do you realize what this could mean?" Sam asked with excitement in his voice. "Maybe there's fresh water."

"*Maybe* is right," she said. "That eagle might be passing over on its way back to the mainland."

Sam reluctantly shifted his gaze to Mack. "If I didn't know better, I'd think you wanted us to fail. That bird could be our guardian angel."

"I don't believe in guardian angels."

"Dante calls guardian angels 'birds of God,'" he said, moving dangerously close to her.

"Dante, huh?" she whispered, too mesmerized to move away. "It surprises me that you'd read Dante."

"A man can be well-read and still down on his luck," he murmured.

"I'm starting to feel like I've hooked up with the Fisher King. What else besides guardian angels do you believe in?" Mack was unable to conceal the tremor in her voice.

"I believe in us," he said. His lips were close enough for her to feel the warmth of his breath on her neck.

Right then she was more afraid of herself than of him. She had to break loose from his magnetic pull. Just how strong he was became apparent when she tried to free herself. His hands caught her shoulders.

"I believe that sooner or later you will, too," he added.

Then, suddenly, he released her, leaving his hands suspended in midair. At that moment, Mack's world divided into two parts—her own flaming desire, and his devilishly handsome pirate's body.

From the dunes Sam saw Mack walking along the water's edge. Her gentle and overwhelming beauty was obvious even from this distance. Behind him the pinkish-orange sun tinted the horizon, casting a mystical spell over the evening. The island was a different place at night, with the nearly full moon rising up over the water, looking cool and luminous.

He watched Mack intently, then began the descent to the beach.

"What are you doing out here?" she asked when he caught up with her.

"Looking for you," he said gently.

He took a deep, calming breath. He felt suddenly, magnificently relieved to be at her side again.

"Okay," she said. "You know where I'm at. Now go away."

He thought he detected a flicker of interest in her intense gaze, and he moved toward her. Nothing could dull the sparkle in her silver-blue eyes. Her skin shone like cream, sparking a desire within him to taste it, to feel its smoothness.

Sam reached out and grasped her hand in his. She hastily tried to withdraw, but he halted her with an iron grip.

"Mack," he murmured. "I want to talk to you."

"You don't have anything to say that I want to hear," she announced defiantly.

"You need to eat. Stop acting like a child and come back to camp with me."

"Go to hell," she said simply.

"If I go to hell, you're going with me," he said, hoisting her up and draping her over his shoulder.

"I don't think so!" She fiercely beat her arms and legs against him.

"Why don't you settle down and tell me what's got you so riled up?" he said, heading toward the dunes with her.

"Don't think you're going to make love to me again, Sam McPhee."

"You talk too much," he told her in a low whisper.

With very little effort, and no further conversation, he carried her back to camp, trying to ignore the silky smoothness of her slender legs. Damn! Those delicious legs of hers were rubbing against a very vulnerable spot. A spot that was beginning to ache like crazy.

When he finally reached camp, he dropped her unceremoniously on her bed.

"I—"

He touched her lips with one finger and discovered that her mouth was a lethal weapon. Sensation shot through him like electricity. "No talking," he murmured.

"I don't like you, McPhee," she snapped.

She was a fighter—he'd give her that.

"I never asked you to like me," he said, in a tone of voice that indicated his patience was wearing thin. "I want to talk to you, and I want you to listen. No more games."

"All right," she said in a small voice.

"Coffee?" he asked.

"*Coffee?* Where—"

"I found packages of instant in your pack."

"You went through my duffel?"

"I figure it's community property until we're rescued," he said coolly. "Cohabitation, I think it's called."

She stared at him, fury sparking in her eyes. "You should have been scouting the island for water, or diving for some of that food that went down with the *Phoenix*. But no, all you can think about is taking advantage of a helpless woman by going through her duffel. You can be a real bastard, McPhee."

"What'll it be?" he asked lightly, offering her a can of instant coffee.

She accepted it with reluctance. He found his focus drawn to her fragile hand, which was cupped gently around the can, pale fingers gently curved, as if holding something delicate.

"I'm diving in the morning," he said, his voice a low rasp. "That's what I wanted to talk to you about."

In the amber glow of the firelight he could see damp traces left by quiet tears on her flushed cheeks. The concern he'd hoped to hear her express wasn't coming. He searched her face for a reaction, but she had assumed a neutral expression. After giving the log a final poke, he turned away from the fire, just as she spoke.

"Why take more chances?" she asked, not a trace of emotion in her voice. "I wasn't suggesting that you risk your life in some daredevil dive."

"You haven't gone and gotten serious about me, have you?"

The look in her eyes indicated that she wanted to slap him.

"I've made you mad," he said innocently.

"You flatter yourself, McPhee," she replied, her words spilling out as smooth as syrup. "The fact is, you have no effect on me whatsoever."

"I don't believe that," he murmured. "You're trembling."

He wasn't talking about goose bumps. The hardness of her nipples was pushing through the thin cloth of her top. Realizing the truth in his words, she glared at him. "I knew you were dangerous, but I underestimated you," she said.

"I think that's the first time you've complimented me."

"Yes, I expect you *would* take it as a compliment," she said too sweetly. "You probably consider yourself a real hero."

She was sharp. Real sharp—shredding him up and spitting him out. He was enjoying MacKenzie Ford's razor wit. She was the first real challenge he'd experienced in years.

"We're down to bare-bones survival here," he said, redirecting the focus of their chat. "I'd like to pretend I'm being heroic, but frankly, I don't see any other choice. Just for the record, if there was another way out, I'd take it."

"Now why doesn't that surprise me?" she said sarcastically. "That's probably the story of your life, taking the back door to escape your problems."

"You have no idea how adept I am at skipping out," he murmured, surveying her, his own large hands cupped around a can of coffee. "I'm just not a system kind of guy."

She tilted her head and crossed her arms. Her hair had come loose from its rubber band, and now the ocean breeze lifted it seductively about her face. There was an unfamiliar stirring in his chest.

"It's possible," he began, "that the boat's two-way could still be working."

"Why haven't you told me?" Mack's voice took on a hint of excitement.

"Anything's possible, but my money is on the battery. We might be able to set up a charge for the cellular phone with it."

"Could you really do that?"

"Like I said, anything's possible."

A rumbling sound filled the air. Sam was halfway to the beach when he saw the *Phoenix* struggling to stay above water.

What was left of the stern had taken on an even more exaggerated tilt. The boat was giving in to the force of the sea. His heart froze as he watched. Any second now the craft might disappear swiftly beneath the waves, taking with it any hope of survival.

The sea claimed a few more feet of her, the waves slapping and hissing. Gigantic bubbles gulped out of the water, demanding every last bit of the *Phoenix,* but the craft held on gallantly. With one final gurgle, the sea gave up for the time being and settled back into its usual rhythm. The crashing of the surf echoed even more loudly now, and Sam knew fate had upped the ante.

The boat hadn't sunk completely. He would still be able to dive. Giddy relief swept through him.

"This is great!" he announced, a sudden burst of laughter rocketing skyward from him. Mack was running to catch up with him on the beach. He swept her, stunned and weightless, into his arms, pulling her roughly against him. "By God, MacKenzie, I'm going to build you a tree house!" He swung her around until they both almost fell down. "Call me Robinson Crusoe...call this crazy...but call us an adventure!"

And then he kissed her, passionately and completely and against her will—at first. The luminescent moon was the only reason he could come up with for his irrational behavior. That and MacKenzie Ford, the highly unusual woman who had cast a magical spell on him.

# Chapter Ten

They had nothing in common. He lived for today. She lived for tomorrow. He craved adventure. She needed stability. He was an out-of-work sixties-style hippie. She was looking for a three-piece-suit type with a nine-to-five job. She wished she had remained in D.C., in the safe world, the one that kept her from longing for the impossible.

Sam hadn't made love to her again down there on the beach, but he had known he could, and that was what was driving her crazy. That, and lying within inches of him. Close enough to hear him breathing. Near enough to smell his manly scent. And wanting him, desiring him, with every inch of her body, with an intensity she'd never known. Things were getting out of control.

"Go to sleep, MacKenzie," Sam whispered in the few inches of darkness separating them.

"I *am* asleep," she snapped.

"You're over there entertaining the same torturous thoughts I am," he murmured. "And if you don't go to sleep, I'm going to come over there and—"

"Drop dead, McPhee."

"You are a passionate woman," he said, in a low and husky voice. "A woman who needs to be tamed. I can see I've got my work cut out for me."

"That you do, McPhee, because I'd prefer to have my legs grow together."

"Like I told you, my sweet, there's no point in fighting it. You're not cut out for a life of celibacy."

Mack ignored him, forcing her eyes shut. The truly awful thing was, he was right. She was tempted . . . very tempted. . . .

"How's THIS for a miracle?" Sam's excited voice roused Mack from a sound sleep into bright sunshine. She bolted to her feet to get a better look as he threw down his find. Lucky Pierre puffed up like a Halloween cat, showing his unhappiness at all the sudden attention.

"Oh, Sam!" she cried out in delight. "Where did you find him?"

"I heard a noise in the trees," he said, stroking the cat, "and after a little investigating, he pranced out and announced himself."

Sam, wearing his tight jeans, was barefoot and without a T-shirt.

"Is the boat gone?" she asked solemnly.

"No," Sam said with obvious concern, "but she broke apart during the night."

"Then you won't be diving," Mack stated matter-of-factly.

"Hell, yes, I'll be diving. Nothing's changed—except the odds."

"You're crazy!" she said, again surprised by this unpredictable man.

"I think you kind of like that, don't you?" he drawled, flashing her a drop-dead-gorgeous pirate's smile. "I think you're starved for adventure."

"You have trouble staying focused, McPhee. This isn't about what I like. It's about surviving."

"Why did you think I was diving?" His voice suddenly turned cold, indifferent. "To impress you, maybe?"

His bronzed skin was stretched tautly over well-developed muscles.

"From now on, here's how it's going to be, McPhee," she said, her voice rising. "We make joint decisions. My life depends on it. Got that? What you do affects me. And in this case, I vote against the dive because..." Dammit! She hated feeding the arrogant man's ego when he was right in the middle of a macho attack. "I stand a better chance of surviving this with you alive."

"Better make up your mind," he said playfully. "Last night you wanted me dead."

"We'll scout the island as soon as I've had my morning coffee— Where are you going?" she demanded. His reply was a wink. "Damn you, McPhee! You can't dismiss me by just walking away!"

He looked gorgeous in his tight Levi's. His muscles were well-defined. It was his ruggedness that attracted Mack, and right now she could almost feel the energy emanating from his body.

"I'm going for a dive," he said simply, continuing across the dunes to the beach.

"Fine," she called after him. "I'm diving with you."

That stopped him. "Like hell you are," he said.

Mack passed him, locking gazes with him as she jogged by. A hint of mischief emerged as a twinkling in his eyes when he spoke. "I'm coming after you, you know."

"I'm counting on it," she purred invitingly.

For the moment, she felt removed from her problems, free, and wonderful. And then she was in the salt water. It quickly engulfed her in an exhilarating rush. Sam entered the water just behind her, and the ocean crashed and roared around them as he worked his way through the water. When he reached her, his hands moved to frame her face. She wanted to press herself to him, to let him protect her, keep her safe, assure her this would all work out. But she couldn't, and it wasn't in his power, anyway.

His face drew closer. He was going to kiss her. It was madness, but she was drunk on the moment, and she wanted his lips more than she wanted anything else—more than she wanted life itself. Her body vibrated with awareness as his hands found their way to her waist. He crushed her to him, rendering her powerless. The longing inside her intensified as she curled her arms tighter around his neck.

"Say it...." Sam whispered, a heavy sigh punctuating his words.

"Say what?" she panted.

"That you want me," he murmured, crushing her to him in a steel grip.

"Never!" she said, but her lips nonetheless parted to receive him.

He deepened the kiss, and she reveled in it, wanting all of him. So intoxicated was she that when the wave hit, it took her by surprise.

The breaker showered its strength on their tangled bodies. They rolled and tumbled together, fighting to free themselves. Then, as suddenly as it had struck, the wave receded. All Mack was aware of was the weight of Sam's body pressing on hers.

She wanted him fiercely, wanted him to make love to her. But she wasn't going to let him. This pirate wasn't cut out for a three-piece suit.

She had had her fling with Sam, and that was all it could ever amount to, she thought regretfully.

"Get off me," she said sourly. "It's not going to happen."

"It already did," he murmured.

"YOU HAVE A GREAT BODY," he called to her.

Sam was back in the water, wading out far enough to start swimming for the *Phoenix*. It wasn't a cold shower, but it would have to do. He didn't care to have Mack see just how much he'd enjoyed the romp with her.

"I'll follow you," she warned him.

"MacKenzie, you feisty devil, I know you're hot for my body, but save your strength this time. I'll take care of you when I get back."

"You don't listen," she said, trudging through the water after him. "I'm coming with you."

"I'll take you with me the next time." His need was powerful and hard to shake, and if she came an inch closer he would be forced to deal with his problem. "Now be a good girl and wait for me back at camp."

"Don't patronize me," she snapped, slapping at the water. "And there won't be a next time."

"You don't expect me to bring everything back in one trip, do you?"

"Don't count on finding me here—*if* you return."

"A taxi ride out of here would cost you half the national debt," he drawled. "I like a woman with a sense of humor."

"This is a big island. We're not joined at the hips."

"Give it up, Mack. What's the point? You know you're crazy about me."

"Don't count on it," she said, in that calm tone. "And don't think I'm going to bury you, either. I hope the fish devour you."

"Me? I plan to stay alive. But don't count on me to save your life again," he said more seriously. "You'll have to do that."

He could see the confusion registering in her eyes. He couldn't let her grow dependent upon him. Not if there was even the remotest chance that it might cost her her life.

He wanted her to live. He wanted that very much.

"YOU'RE A COWARD, McPhee!" Mack shouted. "I want you to return so I can kill you with my own hands."

"That's one hell of a send-off, lady," he growled, in his deepest, most sensual tone. "I'm tempted to turn around and surrender."

But he didn't. And for that, Mack was grateful. She couldn't have resisted—and he knew it. She needed to keep away from him. The man was driving her mad. But, unfortunately, she couldn't escape him. She would be forced to deal with him until they were rescued.

She was beginning to wonder if she had only imagined the other world she'd known. The one with logic and discipline. Any minute now she expected the Tin Man to show up with Toto. It would probably take a tornado to deliver her back to where she came from.

And if Sam didn't walk out of that water within the next five minutes, she was going in after him.

She watched the hands of her watch for the five minutes. Still there was no sign of Sam. Right now there wasn't anyone on the face of the earth she cared to see more than him. She paced. but that didn't help. She sat down. Stood up. Paced again. Nothing helped.

*Make up your mind, MacKenzie.* Half of her wanted him. Half of her rejected the notion. Two extremes, with nothing in between. Just like Sam.

"What else can happen, dammit?" she muttered, flopping down onto the wet sand and dropping her face into her hands.

Mack suddenly realized that Sam's indifferent attitude belied his motives. It was a cover-up. He was risking his life for her again. And he had been trying to force her to face the possibility of having to survive on her own if the need arose. Well, she had no intention of sitting around here and waiting for his body to float ashore. She was returning to camp. The fire needed tending. And there was supper to think about. And nightfall. She hated the dark....

She was halfway to camp when she heard a noise she couldn't identify. She stopped and turned toward the water. And then she saw him, struggling with his load, which he had tied up in T-shirts.

She didn't remember running to him, wading out to reach him, or helping him drag the treasures ashore.

"Why didn't you just drag the *Phoenix* into camp?" she asked playfully. Closer inspection of the cache raised her ire. "McPhee, these are *my* T-shirts!" she said tightly.

"I had to take part of you with me, MacKenzie," he murmured.

Damn him, he was effective. She loved the way he said her name. It was so much nicer than "Mack."

"Yeah? Well, the next time you rummage through my duffel, ask first."

In spite of her anxiety, her anger, she was overjoyed and relieved to have him back. It took everything she had to keep from throwing her arms around his beautiful neck. Beads of water danced on his delicious body like yellow pearls of spilled champagne, tempting her to lick them off.

"Well? Do you approve?" he asked, spreading out the assorted goods.

"What? No can opener?" she said after thoroughly searching through the paraphernalia-laden T-shirts.

"I should throw you across my knee and give you what your father should have given you years ago."

"Leave my father out of this," Mack said tightly.

The spirit of the moment took a drastic plunge. "Hey," Sam said, all traces of mockery gone from his voice. "I didn't mean to upset you."

"You didn't upset me."

"Yes, I did."

Mack opened her mouth to protest, then realized how useless the effort would be. The man had a knack for igniting her anger more quickly than anyone she'd ever met.

"I need some fresh air," she informed him as she turned to leave.

"You've got an entire island filled with the stuff," he murmured, grabbing hold of her arm.

"Exactly!" she snapped. "Now let go of me! I want to breathe it alone!"

She tried to pull away from him, but he only tightened his grip.

"What did I do?" he asked, confusion registering in his dark eyes. "I just risked my life for you."

"I know that," she said indifferently.

"You've got an odd way of showing your appreciation."

"You were saving your own hide, too," she mumbled, looking away. "That should be reward enough."

"Fine," he snapped, releasing his grip on her. "Get some fresh air. Get plenty, because you've got an attitude, lady."

Tears gathered behind Mack's eyes. She blinked and turned away so that Sam wouldn't see them. Then she walked away and never looked back.

THAT WAS THE CLINCHER. He'd just risked his life for her, and all she was concerned about was a damn can opener?

Sam took a deep, calming breath and set out after her. This time she'd headed inland. Anything could happen to her. She might fall. She might step on a rattlesnake. She was smart enough to avoid danger, but this was all unfamiliar territory to her, and he didn't want her ending up injured, considering their predicament.

He didn't have to look far. She was sitting under a nearby sweet gum tree.

"What are you doing here?" she asked with an excess of dignity.

She just stared at him through those huge, icy blue eyes. He could see quite clearly from her expression that she was hurting.

"Looking for you," he said matter-of-factly.

As he neared Mack, he noticed the tear streaks down her cheeks. He knew he'd sometimes been too rough on her, but he didn't have a clue as to what he'd done to provoke this latest incident.

He blamed himself for bringing her to the island. And he understood if she needed to have a good cry. But he also knew better than to offer sympathy right now. Instead, he wanted to fill her with resolve, and he would do it the only way he knew how.

"Out here feeling sorry for yourself?" he mused.

"I despise you."

"Good. What makes you think I like you?"

She looked up at him, confusion mixing momentarily with the hurt in her eyes. He was getting adept at throwing her off guard. And he felt bad for it. In spite of the tough facade she erected, she was delicate and vulnerable.

"Now, if you're through acting like a child," he said flatly, "shall we return to camp?" He offered his hand, but she ignored it. "I brought the groceries. The least you can do is cook them."

"I'm not cooking anything for you."

"Fair enough, but you won't like my cooking." He turned to leave, then said casually, "Watch out for creepy critters."

"Get out of my way," she said, moving past him as though she'd never entertained any notion of remaining behind. "I was looking for Lucky Pierre. He's missing again."

"Damn cat," he mumbled. "He's going to get himself killed courting."

"What?"

"That's what he's doing, you know," he said with a sly grin. "Courting. He'll turn up now and then when it's convenient."

Sam's expression became contemplative as he focused on the next peril, which happened to be the battery on the *Phoenix*. He'd already decided to make certain their situation on the island was completely safe before he re-entered the *Phoenix*. And there was a great deal he could do to secure the camp beforehand...just in case anything went wrong on the dive.

When they were back in camp, he asked, "Is this what you're looking for?" He fished in his jeans pocket and finally pulled out his well-worn Swiss army knife. "Well," he said evenly, "now you have everything you need." He fanned the blades open, then identified each one for her. "You've got your big blade, little blade, screwdrivers, corkscrew—

and can opener. It'll come in handy while you're cooking supper.''

She was impressed, but her response was unexpected.

''It's a beautiful knife, but are any of those blades sharp enough to shave with?'' she asked, a charming curiosity in her voice. It was good to have the old, defiant Mack back.

Sam held a blade between his thumb and forefinger and shaved a small patch from his forearm.

''Take it from me,'' he said. ''It's sharp as hell.'' He dropped down on one knee and took hold of Mack's bare leg. ''Let's see, you probably start at the top.... Am I right?''

Mack glared down at him in protest as he slid his large hand up her smooth leg. He didn't miss the barely noticeable tremor just beneath the satiny smooth skin.

''Why, you wax!'' he announced mischievously.

''What would you know about grooming?'' she snapped. ''Let go of my leg! And while you're at it, you might turn that weapon on yourself. When's the last time your beard saw a razor?''

Sam stood, then noticed her arm.

''Come on,'' he said, ''let me check the wound you got when the boat went down. I brought the first aid kit.''

''It's a little late for that, isn't it?''

''I just put on my doctor's hat.''

"Just how many hats do you have, McPhee?"

More than he cared to admit, although he wished now that he'd been up-front with her from the beginning about being an attorney. There was a part of him now that needed Mack on a level beyond physical desire. Days ago it had seemed to be in his best interests to keep his personal and professional status ambiguous. Now it would be pointless to further undermine her trust in him by divulging those details of his life.

"What?" he said beguilingly. "Tell you, and take away all the mystery? Never."

"I wouldn't trust you—"

He flashed her a grin, but privately he had to admit he didn't trust himself either, not with her. If only she weren't so damn sexy when she turned feisty.

"Tell you what," he said. "Let's put a dressing on that wound, and if I cause you any pain, I'll clean up after supper. Deal?"

"I don't make deals." She stared into the fire for a moment. "Besides, the dressing can wait until tonight."

It was her way of tacitly offering him a truce. Sam gratefully accepted it for now, but he knew that sooner or later he would have to deal with MacKenzie Ford. And that would mean he'd need to put all his cards on the table... every last one of them. And so would she, because he knew she wasn't playing by the rules, either.

A BULLET OF SENSATION split Mack into a thousand different parts when Sam lifted her hair from her neck. One tiny part of her wanted him to keep touching her, while another part of her ordered her to put a halt to it. His hand seared a path down from her head to her shoulder, setting her skin on fire. She was suddenly grateful that it was nearly dark, because she felt flushed all over.

"Okay," Sam murmured, "just concentrate on how much you dislike me, and I guarantee you won't feel any pain."

He abruptly turned to stir the fire. Flames soared skyward before the blaze satisfied him. She enjoyed watching him work. His mind was razor-sharp, which probably accounted for his ability to think ahead. When he finally looked back at her, she was relaxed and entranced by the dancing flames.

"Are you ready?" he asked.

The break had given her a chance to put her defense mechanisms in place, though she still felt an irrational uneasiness over his nearness. "As ready as I'll ever be," she said, in her most professional tone.

He dropped to his knee before her to take a closer look at her wound. The depth and clarity of his dark eyes was devastating.

"Just how I've been wanting you," she said softly.

"You mean close to you?" he murmured.

His strong hands seemed to be seeking out pleasure points. The whole thing was driving her nuts. Worse, she couldn't seem to move. She was mesmerized by desire and fear—fear that he would pull away.

"No, on your knees," she replied tartly.

"Always happy to oblige a lady," he said, a touch of seductiveness in his voice. His hands were skillfully working the kinks out of her shoulders.

"Stop that," she said anxiously. "You're supposed to be tending to my lacerated shoulder."

"Don't rush me," he said, "I'll get to it eventually."

She didn't move. She couldn't.

"I'm enjoying this immensely," he murmured.

She shot him a sidelong glance and caught him looking at her breasts. Each small globe was marble-hard, the nipples standing at attention.

"I have quite an effect on you," he whispered, his mouth close enough for her to feel his warm breath caressing her neck.

"Ah, the male ego," she said primly. "Ouch!" Mack squirmed as he applied the iodine. "Why didn't you warn me?" she said, wrinkling her nose.

"Where does it hurt?" he murmured, and laid his lips against her bare shoulder. He deliberately slid his hands up and down her back.

Mack considered herself a civilized woman. But this was not civilized. "Stop it," she said as his fingers played through her hair.

"You need to learn how to relax," he said in a lazy voice.

*Relax?* How could she? Her safe, dull world had been stripped away by a time-traveling pirate named Sam McPhee. From the moment she'd first laid eyes on him, sitting on the curb at the Potomac Boat Club, she'd felt his pull, but she had fought it, written it off as pure physical attraction. But Mack knew she'd never been attracted to a man in such a way. And now, little by little, bit by bit, Sam was wearing down her defenses. She had to put a stop to it before this pirate captured her.

"I think your problem," he whispered, "stems from your sex life—or lack of it."

"*You're* my problem," she announced, jumping up. "But not anymore. You're not getting your hands on me again."

She straightened her clothes, determined to put an end to this out-of-control desire she was feeling for him, once and for all. It had gone too far already. There was simply no future for her with a man like Sam—just more hurt, more lonely abandonment.

"Okay," he murmured, "there's more than one time-out allowed per game."

"Only someone as irresponsible as you could think of this as a game," she said dryly.

"Brandy?" Sam said, offering her one of the little bottles he had taken from the *Phoenix.* "Go ahead," he coaxed. "I'm the doctor."

She accepted, of course. It felt good to relax. Relaxing was something she had done little of lately. She took a comfortable drink, feeling the brandy's warm, healing effects immediately on an empty stomach.

Sam pitched the empty bottle into the fire. Without another word, he moved next to her and lowered his face to hers, meeting her lips with a burning kiss that could easily have grown into a blazing fire. Mack was determined not to give in this time. She was just having trouble pulling away. Her mouth had automatically opened to accept the thrust of his tongue, which darted against hers, skillfully teasing, withdrawing, tracing a path over her teeth, her lips.

"No...no... No!" She struggled to free herself.

"Why?" he muttered thickly, still trying to press her to him.

"Because I said no! And no means no."

"You can interrupt this," he said angrily, drawing back, "but you can't stop it." He recovered his composure quickly. "It's going to happen. I know it and you know it."

"What I know is that you and I have nothing in common beyond the boundaries of this bizarre situation."

"I see," he said flatly.

"No, you don't see at all."

"Then fill me in. What is it that you're looking for?"

"Not a lot. Just someone stable."

"A neat and orderly life?" Sam said in a clipped tone. "You probably want the white picket fence, too."

"I want a man who gets up and goes to work every day. I want a husband who comes home to his family every night," she said, almost pleading for his understanding. "What's wrong with a neat and orderly life?"

Without warning, Sam closed the distance between them. He wrapped his arms around her, pulling her up against his muscular chest, pressing her erotically against him. It was as though she were drowning. All she could do was cling to him.

"It's boring, my sweet." He breathed the words seductively, totally in control. "You're not cut out for a dull life in a gingerbread house with a three-piece-suit kind of guy who's married to the office while you're left at home, all alone."

"You're the biggest challenge I've ever encountered," she said, surprisingly cool. It had been a struggle riding out the first panic attack, and she felt another one hard on its heels.

"It's nice to know I'm appreciated," Sam drawled.

"Let me put it like this," she said, a little too sweetly. "Never, in all my encounters, have I met a man as flawed as you, Sam McPhee."

She allowed her anger to kick in. It always gave her a sense of power, and right now, more than anything, she needed power to control her undeniable response to the tautly muscled body pressing against hers.

"Want my advice?" she asked, averting her eyes from the pull of his. "Save yourself for some unfortunate woman who might be compatible with you!"

## Chapter Eleven

Sam knew damn well that what MacKenzie Ford needed was him—the kind of man he was now, one who could give her more than an ivy-covered cottage with a white picket fence. A mocking inner voice reminded him of his vow not to become involved. And the undeniable and dreadful fact was that he presently had no means of support, and therefore had nothing to offer a woman.

He opened another brandy and nearly drained the miniature bottle. Mack hadn't spoken to him in more than an hour, and he was certain she wasn't asleep. But he had long since run out of diversions to draw her attention. Despite her height, her small frame and slenderness made her appear delicate and helpless; as she lay curled in a ball, Sam knew she was a bundle of trouble.

"I think you're spoiled," he said, surprised to hear his own thick-sounding voice echo his private thoughts. He knew the admission had lit the fuse of a bomb that would explode momentarily.

*"Spoiled?"* Mack cried, in a voice about three octaves too high.

She drew herself into a sitting position, wide-eyed and alert, stretching her long, delicious legs out in front of her. He'd been right about her lying there playing possum.

"If your ego doesn't devour your brain," she said huffily, "your arrogance will."

Mack usually allowed herself time to think, but this time he'd plainly made a direct hit on all the right nerves. He silently applauded his skill, even while questioning his wisdom. Okay. He'd made better judgment calls.

"What you know about me wouldn't fill up a business card," she said defiantly.

"You're not so hard to figure out," he told her. "You have a pretentious life-style, a trendy car and designer clothes..." She was wounded, he saw it in her eyes, and now he was going in for the kill, because it was the only way he had of striking out at her right now. "You and I are a lot alike," he blundered on, "I'm arrogant, you're pretentious, but they amount to the same distasteful character flaw."

"There's one big difference," she shot back. "You're predictable."

"Life is full of little trade-offs," he said dryly. "Your trouble is that you're looking for stability and adventure in the same pair of arms." He popped open another brandy bottle. "This island trip is the closest you've ever come to a walk on the wild side, isn't it?"

Mack stared at him through the darkness. All he could hear was the faint lapping of salt water hitting the beach, and her breathing. He could see her chest rising and falling in the starlight. The night air had a nip in it, but the temperature was pleasant enough, and he couldn't help wondering why her nipples had turned rock-hard again. The very thought of her soft, warm flesh pressed against him was intoxicating. Still, he was determined to chip away at her resolve.

"The pampered child?" he asked, as if the answer were obvious.

"I was sent to a boarding school when I was twelve, if that's what you're getting at."

She spoke in a monotone, and the animation had left her face. He was beginning to feel like a heel.

He sighed. "I knew it!"

"My father didn't want me . . . and I think it was too painful for my grandmother to look at me."

He scrutinized her critically, then settled back, satisfied that this time he had broken through her fragile facade. But the result was disappointing. She simply sat there in a lonely silence. He fought his overwhelming need to be close to her, to comfort her. Damn. The woman was getting to him. He should apologize, but he couldn't. He wanted to tell her how much he cared about her, but he couldn't. He wanted to tell her how very much he admired her, but he couldn't do that either. Instead, he offered her a tacit truce.

"Coffee?" he said, making a valiant attempt to humble himself.

She remained silent and defeated. And he had only himself to blame. Sam sensed a greater depth to her hurt than could have been inflicted by the words he'd just directed at her. He had reopened an old wound—of that much he was certain.

"Brandy?" he murmured.

She studied him for a moment, then nodded yes. Without a word, she reached for the can he offered her, hands trembling, careful not to let her fingers touch his. He watched as she took a long sip of the mixture of coffee and brandy.

"We were very poor," she said, looking child-like with her slender legs pulled up to her chest. "My mother worked hard to give me the things I needed."

"Aren't boarding schools expensive?" he asked, curious.

"My father put me there when I was twelve," she said stiffly.

She took another deep swallow of her coffee, and he noticed that the brandy had steadied her hands.

"Your father and mother divorced?"

"My father abandoned us," she corrected. "My mother died shortly afterward."

"And you blame your father," Sam said.

"Blame him?" she said sweetly. "You really are presumptuous, McPhee. Cancer makes no distinction." Her voice was little more than a whisper. "No one, not even my father, could have bought a cure for her. No, I don't blame him."

There was something going on behind those big, deep-set eyes, but Sam hadn't a clue as to what it was, except for the wave of sadness that passed over her features.

"Where does your father live?" he asked, wanting to know about every facet of her life. "Are you close?"

"That depends upon what you mean by close," she said, recovering sufficiently to put her defenses back in place. "He doesn't live far from where I reside, but he's a busy man, a self-absorbed man..."

Her voice trailed off, but she'd said enough for Sam to understand the lonely abandonment she felt. There was nothing unusual about the bitterness she harbored, he thought, but she needed to make peace with her father and get on with her life. And he understood that not all men were cut out to raise a daughter by themselves. He wasn't making any judgments just yet.

Still, he wanted to say something, to comfort her. But here he sat, like a tongue-tied adolescent who could only shake his head regretfully as she divulged painful childhood secrets that would have remained buried had he not angered her into talking.

"My mother was a practicing psychologist, so of course she imposed logic on a tragic situation. I only knew I was losing my mother. It made no sense to me."

"So your father was left to raise you," he said logically.

"No," she said emphatically. "A twelve-year-old daughter was not in the scheme of things for him. I never saw him after Mother's funeral."

"Maybe he just wasn't a nine-to-five kind of guy," Sam murmured, tossing the remainder of his brandy into the fire. "I'm not sure that's all bad."

The flames suddenly doubled, tripled, in size, licking at the sky. The bright glow illuminated Mack, intensifying Sam's undeniable awareness of her. His breath caught in his chest at the sight of her.

Mack managed a choked laugh. "So noble, McPhee."

"Noble?" he echoed. "I just don't happen to embrace the theory that a regimented life is the best life. I can't see myself as one of those mindless clones, commuting to and from the office every day of the week, only to wake up one day and find out the boss has swindled you out of your pension fund."

"Is that your excuse for walking out the back door on life's responsibilities?"

He was learning about Mack. She didn't waste bullets. She held her fire for that shot that was certain to knock you down.

"What makes you so certain I did that?"

"If I'm wrong, you can correct me."

"You're beginning to sound like an analyst, and I don't believe in analysis," he said, stirring the fire one last time.

"Well, that's something we agree on. I think it's terrible to pay money you usually don't have to buy a friend who will listen to you complain about all the things that are wrong in your life."

"I fail to see what you would have to complain about anyway. You appear normal as hell to me," he said, using his most seductive tone of voice. "In spite of your absent father."

"Are things always so damn easy for you?" she asked.

Sam rolled over without so much as a sidelong glance at Mack, praying the brandy would kick in and work its magic. "Get some sleep," he said hoarsely. "You're going to need it."

MACK SHUT HER EYES, wishing Sam had corrected her with an announcement that he was a successful entrepreneur.

She wondered how she was going to be able to stand this, sleeping within a few inches of him, knowing that a whole world separated them and that nothing could change that. Beyond that, she knew nothing, was certain of nothing. Except that she would continue to long for the caress of his lips on her mouth, her body, and that she desired him with a hunger completely new to her.

She turned her face into her canvas bed cover, inhaling the musty scent of it. Anything to get her mind off Sam. The wind picked up and rushed past her. She heard Sam's whisper carry through the darkness.

"You all right?" he asked, his words thick and sleepy-sounding.

"I'm fine."

"Can't go to sleep?" he murmured.

"I'm getting there."

At her feet, Lucky Pierre stirred, and she reached for him, pleased that the feline had seen fit to pay her a visit. She lay back, numbed by the thought of numerous reasons she had for ignoring the sensations pumping through her. *I should have stayed home.* But she had not, and so had sealed her fate ... and Sam's.

Mack crept away as soon as Sam was sleeping soundly. She took along a set of clean clothes, glad she'd packed so many pairs of shorts, and all those cool summer tops. She had forgotten to pack extra bras, but her breasts were small enough that she could go without support. Just the thought of being clean, even salty clean, sent ripples of excitement down her spine.

The peaceful surf beckoned. She was dying for a bath, and she needed a breather from a multitude of troubles. The walk to the beach invigorated her. She decided to put her thoughts about the senator on hold. For now, this world belonged to her. She refused to allow anyone to intrude.

Gentle waves licked at her toes, drawing her attention to the ceaseless ebb and flow of the ocean. The beauty of water bathed in moonlight took her by surprise. A wave of exhilaration spiraled through her body, and she hugged herself, breathing in the clean salt air.

She stripped down to her panties, then she discarded them, too, and inched her way into the water until it was up around her legs. The waves gently lapped against her, and she gasped as the cold water crept up her body. She backed away, wet enough for soap, and shivered against the light wind wrapping itself around her. After a good drenching with shampoo, she lathered herself from head to toe. Her skin took on a silky-smooth texture that felt glorious. Satisfied that she was clean, she headed back into the water to rinse off the soap.

"What you're doing is dangerous," came a seductive voice.

Mack's breath caught in her throat. Instinct jerked her around to face Sam, exposing five feet nine inches of naked body clad only in beads of salt water.

Sam's busy eyes were taking in every morsel.

"Stop gawking and turn around," she ordered.

If she'd expected him to obey politely, she'd deluded herself. In a last-ditch effort to salvage her pride, Mack used her splayed hands and arms to cover what she could of her private parts.

"Give me my clothes," she said flatly, not at all surprised to find him before her in a relaxed stance, with the items she desired dangling from his finger.

His eyes sensuously scanned her body. "Come and get them."

"Spare me the juvenile curiosity, McPhee," she said, making an admirable attempt at sounding matter-of-fact. "You've seen it all before."

Her words didn't keep Sam from continuing to look for another long, burning moment. He was right, she realized. Stripping down and bathing on a deserted beach when the only other person on the island was a gypsy pirate was dangerous. The irony was that she had crept out here secretly to avoid his scrutiny.

"You're beautiful," he murmured.

"I'd like some privacy—if you think you've seen enough."

He continued to stand there, rooted to the spot, focused on her. Despite her better judgment, it pleased her to hear his sharp indrawn breath as his gaze traveled the length of her. He showed no intention of moving. He looked like a predator that had just given chase and was now anticipating the feast.

She was thinking she would be unable to withstand his sensuous onslaught a moment longer when, abruptly, his mood changed.

"Get dressed," he said roughly, tossing her clothes to her.

She caught them reflexively. When she realized he'd succeeded once again in making her vulnerable to him, all the passion inside her turned to furious rage.

"Go to hell," she said calmly, too calmly. That calm was an almost sure sign she was about to blow.

What Mack did next surprised even her. She sent her clothes sailing and marched straight toward camp—naked as a newborn baby.

"Wait a minute," Sam called to her. "Aren't you going to dress?"

Mack stopped abruptly and stiffened, but she didn't turn around. She was still naked, still angry, and still vulnerable.

"You've been trying to get my clothes off ever since we met. I'm buck-naked and defenseless on a deserted island. Make up your mind, McPhee."

She told herself she was glad she'd called his bluff, but somewhere, deep down inside her, she knew she would live to regret her impulse. She straightened herself with as much dignity as a naked person could muster and marched away, inwardly reveling in Sam's open admiration of her.

No warning sounded. He just swept her into his arms, from behind, catching her off guard. She tried to yank herself free, but she was no match for his powerful body.

"Put me down!" she ordered in a tight voice.

"Whatever you say," he murmured, deliberately sliding her down the length of him.

She heard herself gasp when she realized he was naked, too. His erection was poised between them, pressing against her, demanding relief. Maddening desire rippled through her, and she realized, with a curious pride and excitement, that this time, she was in command of *his* passions.

"You need a cold shower," she mused.

"Great idea," Sam said, a huskiness in his voice she never heard before. "Come on," he said, pulling her by the hand. "I've never made love in the ocean."

"Oh, no..." she said stubbornly.

"No?" he echoed seductively. "Then why are your nipples hard? And why is your body trembling?"

Her body was betraying her. To protest was useless, and she knew it. The man was stubborn, and crazy to boot.

She experienced a flooding of uncontrollable joy as they ran toward the water.

"Ever been skinny-dipping?" he murmured.

She watched him dive into an oncoming wave, and reluctantly looked away.

"Come on," he urged her.

The next receding wave delivered her into Sam's arms, which clamped around her waist. Excitement glistened in his dark eyes. Another low breaker lifted them, and a ripple of excitement exploded inside her as they floated over the crest of it. Mack felt as though they were about to fly.

"We're too far out," she said, breathless with excitement.

But Sam wasn't listening. He pulled her to him, and for a moment all she could feel was his rock-hard chest pressing against her breasts. She wanted his mouth, but he denied her, that glint of mischief building in his eyes. He slid his hands down her body until he reached her legs, then pulled them around his waist. She could feel his erection pressing against her. Still he held back, not yet joining her to him. He tightened his arms around her, holding her at the arch of her back, and he buried his face in her breasts, licking, biting, teasing, until Mack felt the tremendous, urgent pull at the center of her core demanding relief.

Just when she thought she couldn't withstand the sensuous onslaught a second longer, Sam filled her with himself in one forceful thrust. His hands splayed around her buttocks, forcing her to accept all of him.

He began a tortuous, teasing, gentle rocking that took her to unfamiliar limits, making her shudder with spiraling passion. She arched into him, feverishly exposing herself to the hungry, searching mouth that was determined to taste the pink pearls adorning her breasts. He took one rock-hard nipple in his mouth and suckled until she was writhing wildly on his manhood. She wrapped her arms around his head, forcing him closer, and she moaned as his tongue danced and darted around the sensitive bud.

He lifted his head, and his gaze locked with hers as his thrusting intensified. Euphoria enveloped Mack, and when he launched her on a flight to heaven, she barely recognized her own voice crying out. A pleasure she'd never known drove her to the edge of madness. She was vaguely aware of Sam's hands bracing her hips for the final thrusts, fast and hard and deep, drawing from her yet another climax. This time they cried out together, then held on to each other as the spasms gradually subsided.

Mack wasn't certain if they'd been in the water for minutes or hours. All sense of time had ceased upon their joining. As a new crest of water lifted them, she felt as though they were flying again. The ride lasted only seconds, and then the next swell pitched them onto the beach, crashing water down on top of them.

"Are you all right?" Sam murmured, lying on top of her.

Her gaze found the outline of his bare chest, dim in the scarce moonlight. She knew that as long as he was there she was all right. But he didn't need to know that. She'd slipped away to avoid the temptation of his arms, and here she lay, wrapped up tightly inside them again.

"No! I'm not all right!" she retorted. "And I don't need you complicating my life, McPhee."

"I was just trying to help out," he said in a strained voice.

"I was fine until you came," she snapped. "Now let me up, dammit."

He did. She was still naked, and this time she *ran* all the way back to camp. As quickly as possible, she slipped into clean clothes and then nestled in her bed, determined to be feigning sleep by the time

Sam arrived. The emotions inside her were spinning out of control. She needed time to think.

Mack had no intention of relinquishing her old world, the one she had left behind, the one she could depend on. Sam would never fit into the existence she'd carved out for herself. He had too much zest for life to be squeezed into a regimented world.

But life without him now also seemed impossible... She shuddered inwardly at the thought, and finally decided to deal with it in the morning. The real shock for her was the realization that for the first time in twenty years, a man other than her father dominated her heart. Mack knew her life had changed forever.

SLEEP HAD BEEN a long time coming for Sam. Which was strange, considering the fact that he'd just experienced the most wonderful lovemaking of his entire life. He'd relived it a hundred times, then finally succumbed to the numbed sleep of the satisfied lover.

How Mack had managed to end up in his arms during the night mattered less to him than what it felt like to have to release her the next morning. All through the predawn hours, he had lain there trying to apply logic to their situation—without success. He knew she wanted the kind of man he used to be, the kind of man he never intended to be again. And he wanted her any way he could get her. He didn't know exactly what he was going to do about MacKenzie Ford, but he did know he wasn't going to let her go.

At first light, he eased out of bed, careful not to wake Mack, who was comfortably snuggled next to him, unbeknownst to her. He'd made a decision during the night to dive for the battery. He had to take some of the items from the wreckage. She wouldn't like it, but survival was still number one on their agenda. He was taking the easy way out by leaving Mack in camp, asleep, while he made the dive.

Sam quietly left camp and trudged toward the water, straining to see if the *Phoenix* was still in sight. Relieved to find the wreck holding, he headed straight for it. The breakers appeared gentle this morning, at least compared to yesterday's pounding ones. Even so, the vast Atlantic carried strength enough to sweep him *and* the *Phoenix* out to sea. He felt humbled by its immensity, its tenacity.

It was possible that their survival depended on this dive. The battery might be all that stood between them and rescue. Sam tried to marshal his churning thoughts. He crossed the dunes and headed out over the sloping beach to the water, ready to pick up the gauntlet thrown down by fate.

He shifted his thoughts to the chore at hand. The boat's battery would be heavy. And deadweight.

His best bet might be to secure it to driftwood and float it in.

"Sam?" Although Mack whispered his name, it seemed to echo as if she had shouted it.

Sam stopped and turned to greet her. He admired her as she marched up to him, but said nothing for a moment. She stared at him, her cheeks flushing with color that matched the early-morning dawn.

"I don't believe this," she said. She looked up at the sky, giving an odd, curt laugh. "How could you do this to me?"

"What?" Sam said.

"Leave me without a word."

Sam put a finger to her lips. He loved the pouty expression her mouth assumed when determination motivated her. His gesture brought only a temporary reprieve. The moment he lowered his hand, her lips were moving again.

"You had no right to try to sneak off without so much as discussing this dive with me."

"It was my decision to make," he said. "I'm trying to get you off this island, dammit. You might keep that in mind."

"That's what makes it my business. You don't have to do this," she said. "These heroic deeds are purely self-serving. Don't you think I see through your little ego trips?"

"Okay, I'm doing this because of *us,* because I like living, because it's the only way to survive this situation."

"We'll figure out something else," she said, suddenly sounding desperate. "You don't have to do this, Sam."

Why did she have to make this so difficult? He admired Mack's tenacity, but right now it was tedious. She hated to give up, he knew that, but it was senseless to argue. When he backed away from her, her eyes took on a solemn look. It was sheer agony for him to pretend a polite distance that he didn't feel, when all he wanted was to pull her into his arms and tell that he loved—*Whoa, McPhee!*

"What makes you so sure I won't return?" he said.

"Because you're tempting fate."

"I think you'd actually miss me," he said, all the arrogance back in his tone.

A smile crossed her face as she considered the possibility. "You grow on a person."

Sam thought his heart would bust through his rib cage as he closed the distance between them. He gripped her shoulders and pulled her to him. Her body was totally responsive to his demands. She tilted her lips up to meet his, closing her eyes.

"Hold that thought," he said. "You haven't seen the last of me."

To her obvious surprise, he released her without so much as a kiss on the cheek. Then he turned and headed down the beach toward the wreckage.

"Damn you, McPhee!" Mack called after him. Already the surf was beginning to drown out her voice.

He tossed her a glance and laughed. "You're crazy about me!"

"You coward!"

"We'll drink to that when I return!"

He wondered if she had any idea how difficult it was for him to leave her this way, perhaps never to return. She would hate him. Yet he knew her anger would fuel her need to survive—with or without him. He would apologize for this when he returned. What mattered to him now was that she had cared enough to try to stop him.

"I despise you!"

"We'll get friendly later," he said, flashing her a seductive grin.

SAM WAS RIGHT about the dive, of course, but Mack hated to acknowledge that fact. At any rate, she didn't intend to watch fate toy with her future, so she headed back to camp. The extent of her opposition embarrassed her now, but she had been too upset, too eager to keep him—she, the aloof MacKenzie Ford.

Back at the camp, she sat in front of the fire for a long time. Only the hammering waves filled the silence. Lucky Pierre had shown up, and he was dining daintily on a can of tuna that she had opened with Sam's Swiss army knife. How that knife suited him, she thought, with all of its various facets. She wondered if she would ever come to know and understand the many sides of Sam McPhee.

Overhead the gulls cried. Mack finished her coffee and watched as a mass of clouds snuffed out the sun. The sky went dark and menacing for a brief moment, and then the light returned. Mack stirred the fire. Forty minutes had elapsed since Sam had left.

For an instant she caught a movement overhead. She dropped her head back, peering into the sky, squinting to focus without the benefit of her missing glasses. An eagle circled high above, its wings dark against the bright blue pockets between the fluffy clouds. She watched as the magnificent bird descended in tight, even spirals from the blue, then began to climb again. Then it came nearer with more circles and spirals. It was almost as if the eagle were challenging her to follow it.

The cat had crawled into her lap and turned on its motor. "You hold down the camp," she told him. "I've got some investigating to do."

SAM POPPED out of the water, gasping for air. The battery rested on a piece of driftwood, secured there with rope and his T-shirt, which he had filled with more bottled water. All that remained of the dangerous feat was to float the battery to shore. He could manage that.

Within minutes he was swimming toward the island with the rope tied around his waist. He felt fire inside his lungs. Still he pushed his body against the water, making his way to safety—and Mack. At last he could feel the ocean floor. Just a few more steps...

When he collapsed onto the sand, his lungs were bursting, but he didn't care. He had the battery. He had water. He had bought them a little more precious time. For a moment he just lay there, waiting for the fire in his lungs to go out.

At the very least, he'd expected a welcoming committee, but when he finally saw Mack running across the dunes to reach him, his disappointment at her initial absence dissipated.

"Sam!" she called out. "Follow me!"

"But...the battery—I retrieved the ship's battery..." Mack was already running inland. "You're crazy! You know that, lady? Crazy!"

"Come on," she said, turning back one last time.

He did. Mack ran inland, turning the pursuit into a chase that entailed ducking, dodging and jumping. She continued on without hesitation until finally she stopped, out of breath but exhilarated.

"What's your surprise?" Sam asked, trying to catch his own breath.

"Look at that tree," she said, "and tell me what you see."

"A loblolly."

"Anything else?"

Sam studied it carefully, beginning at its base until finally he reached the top, where he spotted the eagle. "I can't believe you located it," he muttered.

"Believe it," she said, her voice filled with enthusiasm. "It's nesting here."

"They mate for life," Sam said. "So there should be another one—unless it's dead."

"How's Captain Hook for a name?" she asked, her face breaking into a grin.

"We don't know if it's a male," Sam said.

"I just thought the name fit."

"This means there's got to be fresh water around here somewhere," Sam said.

"That's my surprise," Mack replied excitedly. She hurried across a clearing to show him. "Come and see. It's a freshwater pond. Of course, we'll need the purification tablets from the first aid kit."

"I wouldn't have thought it," Sam said in a stunned voice. The freshwater pond was about twelve feet across. He searched until he found a scrawny branch he could use to test the pond's depth. "Nearly six feet deep," he said.

"You won't believe what you can see from the top of a tree here."

"You've already climbed one?" he asked.

"While you were diving."

Driving wind had banked up sand around the bases of most of the surrounding trees, giving access to their lowest branches from the ground. Mack demonstrated her tree-climbing ability by hoisting herself onto the low arm of an oak.

Sam admired the graceful movements her sleek body made as she climbed up the thick old tree. Once she had secured herself on a branch, she scaled the remainder of the trunk like a cat after prey.

"Coming?" she called down.

He followed, discovering that the spidery branches provided grips. He inched toward her on what appeared to be a solid branch. But every time he moved closer to her, she eased farther away, until finally there was no more branch.

"Looks like you're at the end of your rope," he murmured.

"Think again, McPhee!"

If he'd expected Mack to surrender to him, he'd deluded himself. Feet first, she plunged into the water below. She reappeared in a matter of seconds, pearls of water glistening on her smooth skin.

Mack eyed him now with renewed excitement. The chase had become a game, but Sam no longer knew if he was the hound or the rabbit.

"How's the water?" he asked.

"Perfect," she called, disarming him with a rueful grin. "Why don't you test it yourself?"

Which of course he did, diving in without another word. When he surfaced, Mack was retreating to the shoreline, scrambling to get out. Sam caught her by one ankle, pulling her off balance. She fell backward into the water, but not before he caught a glimpse of her breasts under her wet T-shirt. Treading water, Sam grabbed hold of her around the waist, pulling her body against his.

"Give up?" he asked.

"Never!"

She caught hold of his shoulders, using them to catapult her toward the middle of the pond.

"Don't count on escaping," he said, exploding out of the water in a sleek dive.

He almost captured her, but she slipped under the water. Again he dived, catching her close to the bottom. This time Mack held on to his shoulders, riding him up to the surface. She was gasping for air when they broke the face of the water.

"You lose," Sam murmured against her mouth, lacing his fingers through hers to pull her into shallow water, where they could stand up.

"I don't think so," she whispered.

As she slid into his arms, a spiral of anticipation shot through Sam. It was as though the water had joined them in the same world, a world without yesterdays, without tomorrows. A world where pure, surging excitement ruled as they clung to each other in passion. Everything in this world was sweet and soft and good.

Sam covered her mouth with his own, feeling her gasp with pleasure as he deepened the kiss. Ripples of pleasure fluttered in his stomach, swelling his manhood as it pressed against her. He lifted Mack up until she was high enough to lock her legs around him. His hands moved under her T-shirt, up her taut stomach until he was cupping the small mounds of flesh that had been driving him crazy through the flimsy fabric.

For a moment they regarded each other across the inches that separated them.

"Stop," Mack said, her breath ragged.

*"Stop?"* he echoed, dazed by the thought of turning back now.

She took a deep breath, and he watched the rising and falling of her breasts. Then she was pushing him away.

"Fine," he said tightly. He dropped her into the water and pulled himself out. "But stay away from me, MacKenzie Ford. Do you hear me? Stay away."

## Chapter Twelve

Before Mack opened her eyes, she knew this day was going to be different. Since the incident at the pond, Sam had changed. For the remainder of yesterday, he'd spoken only when necessary, spending all his time gathering driftwood from the wreckage and hooking up the cellular phone to the ship's battery. And Lucky Pierre was missing—again.

She was determined to stand her ground. There would be no more lovemaking with Sam until she could figure out what was going on between them.

In theory, it was a wonderful notion—having fate strand you on a deserted island along with a deliciously handsome pirate. In reality, life had to be taken into account. If Sam could make the cellular phone work, she would be on her way back to D.C. and a hot shower. She waited on pins and needles while he checked the small machine.

"What do you like on your pizza?" he asked, flashing her a wicked smile. "Of course, they might not deliver this far from Virginia Beach."

"Sam!"

Excited, Mack jumped across the distance separating them and threw her arms around his neck.

"You did it!" she shouted. "Who will you notify? The coast guard? You could call a television station—they have choppers. Wait! The police have rescue craft."

She pulled away, wanting to search his face for a reaction.

"I'm not calling anyone," he said flatly. "If you need a taxi, there's the telephone."

Mack sucked in a breath, as if she'd been kicked in the stomach. "I don't understand," she mumbled.

"It's not complicated," he said. "I'm not trading paradise for the rat race I left behind."

He used a deliberately casual tone. If he was feeling a hint of urgency, she couldn't tell. This was a new, aloof Sam, and she didn't understand him. For a moment, he didn't look at her. He studied the sea, wild and free in the distance, as wild and free as she suspected he wanted to be.

"You can't mean that," she said at last.

"Oh, but I do."

Apprehension tightened like a knot in her stomach, and she tried to calm herself. All he had done was tell her that he had decided to remain on this remote island. No one was holding her prisoner. She was free to go.

"You'll need this," he said, handing the cellular phone to her.

His hand felt cold and icy, and the sinking sensation she experienced in her stomach made her want to cry. But she couldn't—not just yet, anyway. She pressed the phone to her ear. To her amazement, there was a dial tone. It was faint, but it was buzzing nonetheless. She turned off the phone and looked at Sam.

"Why don't you do something about your life," she demanded in a nervous voice, "instead of running away from it?"

"You don't get it," he said. "I *am* doing something."

"What does that mean?"

"It means I'm getting rid of the problem."

"No. It means you're getting rid of the rules. We all have to play by the rules, Sam."

He held himself erect, straightening his broad shoulders and cocking his head sideways.

"That's right," he said defiantly. "My island. My rules."

"You're just mad over what happened at the pond yesterday," she said impatiently.

He shot her that pirate's grin. "Poor Mack," he said. "You really do believe that, don't you?"

"Don't condescend to me...not after everything that's happened."

"Then don't patronize me! I know what I'm doing."

"I'm not staying," she blurted.

"Who invited you?"

The old Sam was back, the arrogant, mischievous one. She didn't know whether to celebrate or cry.

"You don't conquer a place like this," she pleaded. "You inhabit it like an occupying army. At best you make an uneasy truce with it." She pointed toward their water supply. "You've been rationing water like its our last gallon of gas and there's a carload of murderers chasing us. What's changed? We're under siege here. The water purification tablets can't hold out forever."

Sam's extraordinary eyes glowed. "Tell your boss I decline his offer. Better yet, *I'll* tell him. Who is he?"

THE MOMENT OF reckoning had arrived. Mack acknowledged his question by lowering her gaze, but said nothing. She managed a rueful smile—probably in an attempt at buying time, Sam thought.

"It's an easy question, Mack," he pressed. "Who hired you to acquire the island?"

"Don't do this, Sam," she said, her voice almost a whisper. Though faintly audible, he still detected the nervous tremor in her tone. "In the end, nothing will change . . . except us."

"Indulge me," he said in a deliberately arch tone.

"All right. What do you want me to tell you, Sam?"

"The truth would do nicely," he said calmly.

"A very powerful U.S. senator wants your island," she began cautiously.

"Why would a senator want a barrier island?"

"That's why I wanted to visit the island with you," Mack said, looking embarrassed. "I suspected something was up when the senator's law firm called me to make the acquisition."

"You've got my attention."

She rolled her lips together and squeezed her eyes shut. "The notion that a U.S. senator wanted a deserted island piqued my curiosity. Then, on the *Phoenix,* I read an article about the senator's dilemma over selecting a garbage dump site in Virginia. Sam . . . he plans to turn your island into a garbage dump."

"What's the senator to you?"

"One of the bad guys," she said softly.

"That's all?"

"I've been investigating him for months."

"That's costing someone a truckload of cash. Who's bankrolling this?"

"It's my own investigation."

"You're lying," he said tightly.

"I'm a concerned citizen," she shot back. "And watch who you call a liar."

"In this country you're innocent until proven guilty. What do you think this senator is guilty of?"

"He's trying to steal *your* property for taxes."

"That's legal," he said, challenging her. "People line up to do it."

"Maybe, but he's probably the only one who plans to turn the island into a dump site. The environmental people would jump on it, and so would the media. Don't you see? We've got a bald eagle to consider."

*"We?"* he echoed skeptically.

"I'll help create a scandal."

"A scandal?" He studied her. "You'll lose your commission."

Sam wanted to think this was about him and not the senator, but he knew better. What did he expect? They were as good as connected to civilization again. She no longer needed him.

"It's a small price to pay for a big fish like the senator." She pleaded with her ice-blue eyes. "Media attention would count the most. The press would set the forces loose—lobbyists, conservationists, pressure groups, lawyers, people of influence."

Sam remained silent, thoughtful, playing catch-up. He felt a rush of excitement, something that had been missing from his life for a long time. By

God, he'd do it. He'd found paradise on this island. He wasn't in any hurry to leave—not without a fight.

"We'll only be buying time," he said, almost to himself. "We'll have to alert the environmentalists. If the island's to be saved, they'll have to get involved."

"Don't you think I know that?"

He continued to study her. "Okay," he said finally.

"Partners?" she asked, extending her hand.

It felt soft and warm. Her grip was strong, and he wanted to pull her against him and tell her that he loved her. He wanted this woman with an intensity he'd never felt before.

"Partners," he said roughly.

Yes, he wanted to be partners—life partners. But he couldn't tell her that yet. Instinct warned against it, and these days he tuned in to his gut feelings.

HAD SHE MADE the right choice? Or had the clear island air clouded her thinking? Mack questioned her motives. Somehow the senator no longer seemed so imposing. Entire days had passed without so much as a thought of him. All those years he'd been larger-than-life in her eyes, but now, with Sam filling her thoughts...

Life had been so simple before....

"All that's left is to pack," she said.

Sam expelled a long breath. "What the hell are you talking about?" His voice was harsh with confusion. "I'm not going anywhere."

"But I thought—"

"You thought I would turn tail and follow you right back to D.C.? I'm not going anywhere," he said stubbornly.

*How could you fall in love with a pigheaded—?* She swallowed, finally admitting it to herself. She'd fallen hard for this time-traveling pirate. So what was next? Where was the time machine? *Get a grip, MacKenzie,* she told herself.

"I'll implement my stalling tactics from right here," he said smugly.

"Are you planning on using carrier pigeons?" she snapped looking around. "There isn't a mailbox in sight. I don't see any reporters popping up out of the sand, either."

"No," he agreed. "But they'll come when the news breaks."

"What news? The story of two shipwrecked people would be lucky to make the 'News in Brief' section."

If she had any sense at all, she'd leave right now.

"Forget about Virginia," he said. "The federal government will have the last say. Senator Anderson knows that. The only chance we have of succeeding is to hit him at the federal level."

"He's in a very powerful position as chairman of the appropriations committee. His name won't be on the moving van, but he will see to it that Captain Hook is removed. I know this man. He'll argue that the rodent population from the dump will benefit the eagle."

"I've thought of that."

"You're not making sense. The island reverts to the senator in a matter of days for taxes."

"Not if I secede from the Union."

"*What?*"

"You heard me," he said.

The idea was totally absurd, which was what made it funny. Mack broke out laughing.

"I didn't intend it as a joke."

"But . . . you . . . you can't do that."

"The South did it."

"But they were serious!"

"And so am I," he said. "I just need time to get an environmental group interested in the land. And I need publicity." He paused. "What do you think?"

"Secession is crazy! The FBI might even get involved. You could be arrested. And the senator will probably laugh you off *his* island."

"Life is crazy," he said. "I'll take my chances."

"We'll lose, Sam."

"Then you're in?"

"I don't believe for one minute that we can really secede—but we can buy time." A spear of excitement raced down her spine. "You know, use it as a stall tactic. The press would have a field day with it—'Man secedes from Union to commute death sentence for bald eagle nesting on potential dump site.' McPhee, you might have something."

"This place grows on you, and I'm not yet ready to let go of it."

*And what about me?* Mack wanted to ask, but instinct advised her not to. Not yet, anyway.

"We still would have to deal with surviving," she said.

"It wouldn't be easy," Sam said.

"No hot showers."

"No shelter."

"Don't try talking me out of it," she warned. "Once I make up my mind, you can't budge me."

"Why would you want to stay?" he asked, studying her through narrowed eyes.

"I believe in the importance of wilderness. It's worth protecting—for our children. Not mine and yours... What I mean is... it's the finest legacy of all to pass on."

"Just like that? You're a conservationist, and you want to stay on for the cause?"

"I've got an interest at stake here, too."

But the fact that years of hating someone she barely knew might finally culminate in his ruin no longer held the same meaning for Mack. The island was growing on her, too. Meeting Sam was turning out to be the best thing that ever happened to her; paradoxically, it was also the worst, since nothing could come of a relationship built on lies.

"My laptop has a built-in modem. With the cellular phone, I can access Washington. Have you ever heard of public domain? By tapping into the library's reference records, I can pull out dial up codes for the press, the environmental agencies ... even the good senator."

But this wasn't about the senator anymore. He was no longer as important as Sam. And if Sam could salvage the island somehow and stay on here, maybe she would be able to see him again. She managed a tight smile. For a brief moment, she struggled against the reality of the arrangement she'd just made.

"We'll need a plan," she said.

"The secession tactic will buy us time to put pressure on the senator through the press."

"I don't know about this, Sam.... Do you think it will work?"

"Seceding from the Union? Of course not. But if I can embarrass the senator—"

"Then you'll get his attention," she suggested, interrupting him.

"Precisely," he said. "First we send the notice of secession, using your computer. Then we call an environmental group to make them aware that a bald eagle is nesting on an intended dump site."

"I know of a group," she said.

"What's their name?"

"The Nature Preserve."

"That's good. When we go public, I want all the networks notified. Your press list should include the *Washington Post* and the *Virginia newspapers,* and any other media outlets you can think of." He paused and scrutinized her. "Are you prepared to fight?" he asked suddenly.

"To the end."

# Chapter Thirteen

"Close your eyes!" Sam said when he woke Mack the next morning. "I've got a surprise."

"Unless you're going to tell me that a helicopter is coming to our rescue, don't bother me," she said in an sleepy voice. "Yesterday, I notified every environmental agency in D.C., the media, not to mention the good senator's office. Today I'm tired."

"Come on," he persisted. "Get up."

"Just show me and leave," she said, pulling the sail over her head.

"I'm counting to three, then I'm throwing you in the ocean. Are you always this lazy?"

She tossed back the cover and flopped over onto her back. She looked flushed and inviting. He knew getting this close to Mack put him in the danger zone. The web of attraction between them was continuing to build, making it more difficult every day to keep his distance from her.

"I am not lazy!" Mack protested, bolting to a sitting position. "All right—what is it?"

"Will you be patient?" he said. "You're as inquisitive as a child."

Of course, that energy was exactly what appealed to Sam so much in Mack's personality. She looked beautiful, even this early in the morning, as she followed him inland. She stumbled, and he reached out to catch her.

"How much farther?" she asked, subtly pulling away from him.

"Do you always complain this much?"

"I've never been shipwrecked before."

"Okay," he said, "don't move—and don't open your eyes until I tell you to open them."

"Are you always this bossy?"

"Only with willful women."

Sam made easy work of climbing up the rope ladder and onto the platform. If there had been a threshold, he would have carried her over it.

"Open your eyes," he called down.

She did, but they clouded up with tears so quickly that he wondered if she could really see enough to appreciate what he had done.

"What are you crying for? I realize it's not finished, but another day and I'll have the rails up, and a table and bench—"

"You don't understand," Mack muttered between hiccups and sobs.

He eased down the rope ladder and closed the distance between them, pulling her next to him. She just stood in his embrace, crying, her hands cupped over her face.

"Will you tell me what's wrong? If you're thinking this is too permanent—"

"Will you shut up! I think it's the most wonderful tree house in the world. It's just that . . . it's the first tree house anyone ever built for me."

"Is that all?" he murmured, wrapping his arms around her tightly enough to feel the entire length of her body pressed against him. "I thought we could move in right now. And look over here. I plan to rig a shower for you from the pond. And do you remember that piece of metal I salvaged from the Phoenix?"

She nodded yes.

"We can use it to build small fires in the tree house by elevating it with rocks."

"You're a genius, McPhee. My very own Robinson Crusoe tree house," she said in a husky voice.

For a brief moment, a light flickered inside Sam, a light that had burned out a long time ago. Happiness—that was what it was.

They were living out a fairy tale. And that was the hard part. Their story could have only one ending, and Sam didn't want to face it or think about it. The island was slated to go on the auction block in a matter of days, and no one had bothered to respond to their notices. And that wasn't the only thing getting to him. He had to admit, he missed the amenities of the city—restaurants, the theater, sweets....

But the thought of losing MacKenzie Ford was breaking his heart. If only he could buy some time with her, until he figured out what to do with the rest of his life...

The cellular phone was ringing, and Sam decided to be the one to answer it.

Civilization burst into his ear with a bang.

"Senator John Anderson here," said the gravelly voice on the other end. "Put Sam McPhee on the line."

"This is Sam McPhee," he said, cupping the receiver with his palm to whisper to Mack who was calling.

The blood drained from her face. Sam figured it was the shock of actually receiving a response. He hadn't seriously entertained the notion of the senator himself responding.

"Good. I'll get right to the point," the senator said. "The federal government doesn't take kindly to pranks, McPhee."

"This is no prank, Senator."

"Well, you, uh...you can't do this."

"I'm exercising my constitutional right to withdraw from the Union, sir," he said, looking to Mack for her reaction. "I can secede—that's democracy."

"This isn't the land of Oz," said the senator.

"Great place, though, huh?"

"Why are you doing this?" the senator demanded.

"To force you into the open with your plans to turn my island into a dump site."

The silence on the line seemed to stretch interminably.

"You've been misinformed," the senator finally said. "And I'm a busy man."

"So am I, Senator. And right now I've got an appointment with an environmental agency. You'll be hearing from me. Check your local newspaper, and tune in to the television."

"Wait—"

But Sam didn't wait. He hung up quickly. He had some tall threats to follow up on.

"Wait a minute, Sam," Mack called after him from the tree house. "The phone is ringing again."

"You answer it this time," he called back.

"Sam, wait!" Mack placed her hand over the receiver. "It's a reporter from a Virginia paper—a Mr. Quinn."

Sam climbed back up, and she handed him the phone.

"Mr. Quinn," he said in a take-charge voice. "It's my understanding that you're the investigative reporter."

"Whose understanding would that be?"

"Sam McPhee's."

"What do you want from me, Mr. McPhee?"

"I own a small piece of real estate, a deserted island, twenty miles off the Virginia Beach coast."

"If you're a prank solicitor, you could be violating federal laws."

"Mr. Quinn, do you know the U.S. senator from Virginia who heads up the appropriations committee in congress?"

"Senator Anderson? Of course. What's your connection to Senator Anderson?"

"The senator needs a dump site to cure Virginia's garbage problem, and he thinks my island is the answer."

"You're wasting my time, McPhee. Make your point."

"A lone bald eagle is nesting on the island."

"Have you located the nesting site?"

"Yes."

"Hmm. We might be interested in covering the eagle's nest. Maybe we'll be able to send a photographer."

"A *photographer?*"

"We're always interested in photographing an endangered species."

"But what about the story?"

"What story?"

Sam had never considered himself a coward, but he didn't want to tell Mack that their efforts had been in vain. No one was interested. He hadn't really expected Washington to take him seriously about seceding, but he had hoped to gain publicity from it for his island and for Captain Hook. He could feel Mack's eyes watching him as he slapped the tiny phone shut.

Five minutes later, he was walking along the beach, alone, facing the inevitable. This was the end of everything—the island, the bald eagle, Queeny, Lucky Pierre, even Mack.

Unless, of course, she was in love with him, too.

THE PHONE RANG all day. Straightening resignedly, Mack tentatively admitted that Sam might be right about throwing in the towel.

It was dusk when he returned. Clearly exhausted, he sank down to rest at the crude table in the tree house. The colors in the western sky were altering from pink to red.

"It's starting to sprinkle," he murmured.

The rain was soft and even at first, but it quickly turned to pounding sheets.

"At least the mosquitoes won't be biting tonight," Mack said, trying to maintain a light mood.

"Stay here," he told her. "I'm going after the canvas. I washed it today, and it's hanging out to dry—or was—below."

It was strange, Mack thought, that someone with whom she had so little in common could be so comforting. She pondered the topic of Sam's life and wondered why he deliberately avoided it. But her thoughts were interrupted by the phone.

She had hung up by the time Sam returned with the canvas.

"What is it?" he asked.

"The Nature Preserve is coming to rescue Captain Hook tomorrow," she said.

"Just like that?" he asked. "Do you realize how difficult it will be to catch that eagle?"

"It's easier to rescue him than it is to take on a U.S. senator. They buy land to protect ecosystems for the plants and animals that inhabit them, but buying the island is out of the question."

"What did you tell them?"

"What could I tell them? I'm glad the eagle's getting rescued."

"Whose side are you on, anyway?" he snapped.

"We tried, Sam."

"You can spare me the pity, because you've got this thing all wrong," he said defiantly. "Frankly, I was tiring of this place. Too much of a good thing always sours."

His words surprised her so much that at first she couldn't answer. But the confusion passed as anger filled her.

"So...just like that," she said, snapping her fingers. "You change your mind and want to bail out?"

"No," he said flatly, "it's been coming on gradually."

The answer shocked her at first.

"You could have told me, Sam," she said in a whisper.

"Told you what?" he asked.

"I'm beginning to understand you," she said tightly. "I thought it was life you were afraid of, but it's not that. It's you."

## Chapter Fourteen

"What do you say we celebrate?" Mack said.

Although it had taken several people most of the day, the Nature Preserve had succeeded in capturing Captain Hook, and Sam had succeeded in cajoling Mack into a decent mood. But now it was over. A television station had caught wind of the story, and, first thing in the morning, it was sending a chopper for them.

"Celebrate what?"

"The end of an exotic adventure."

"Why not?"

"We're the recipients of a gourmet dinner for two," she said in an attempt to sound cheery. "Compliments of the Nature Preserve."

It was their last night together. That was what Mack was trying to say. Tonight she intended to squeeze enough pleasure out of the island and Sam McPhee to last a lifetime. Because deep down,

Mack knew this was the last time she would see him—or this piece of paradise. And she intended to make the most of it.

"Sit down," she ordered him.

"Mack...I don't want to talk right now."

"Who said anything about talking." Mack extracted the sharpest blade of his Swiss army knife.

"What are you doing with *that?*"

"Since dinner is special tonight," she said, sizing him up, "I'm going to shave you."

"Are you now?" he murmured, the gleam back in his eye.

"I'm holding the knife."

"Then I guess you are," he said in a seductive tone.

"I want to see what you look like...what you *really* look like."

Mack hadn't counted on feeling so awkward as she moved next to Sam. His nearness was so intense, so intoxicating. Although he made no move to touch her, she felt a tremor just beneath his skin, felt his irregular breathing, felt the warm flush on his face.

Her hands somehow managed to move deftly, and slowly his beard fell away, revealing a Sam McPhee she didn't recognize. His boldly handsome face smiled back at her, and she inhaled sharply. He appeared even more self-confident with his new look. It took her a moment to collect herself.

"Well?" he asked, still capable of flashing a pirate's smile. "What do you think?"

"I—I don't know what to say," she mumbled.

*Liar.* She knew damn well what to say. He was achingly handsome. She'd set out to make this a night that would last forever, and she'd succeeded admirably. And all she needed to know from him now was what he had in store for the two of them for the rest of their lives.

"How about some wine?" she said huskily. "I don't know the vintage, or how good it is...."

"Once I considered wine drinking an artistic experience," Sam murmured, "but tonight there's no such thing as bad champagne."

"No second thoughts?" Sam asked in a husky whisper, and lifted his glass.

"None," she said softly, draining her wine.

"Lie down," her pirate said, and she obeyed.

One last time Mack was escaping reality and slipping into her pirate's fantasy world. She had known other men, but Sam had been the first to really know her body. He was working magic with his hand, generating moist heat from her core.

He had branded her with his mouth, and now she wanted the fire from his lips on every inch of her body. He didn't disappoint her. Kneeling between her parted thighs, he paused to look into her eyes.

Missing was the teasing laughter in his gaze, replaced by a sexy look that told her he was going to kiss her thoroughly... all over.

She could feel his ragged breathing, evidence of his desperate need of her. As soon as his lips touched her, shooting flames danced through her. The tip of his tongue flicked across the folds of soft skin, nearly driving her mad, pushing her to the limit too quickly. She struggled, but her adrenaline, her blood, her heart, all were racing.

He must have felt her shaking, because he returned to her side, pulling her into his arms and pressing his mouth against her lips. She spiraled higher and higher in the most exquisite climax she'd ever experienced. And then he eased himself into her softness, cautiously at first, then gradually harder as she arched to meet each thrust. Again shudders rippled deep within her.

She clung to him while he found release, desperately holding on, wondering if he, too, was aware that time was short and fleeting. All too soon, her dream would be at an end.

MUCH LATER Mack lay against Sam's taut body, forcing herself to breathe slowly and carefully, afraid a sob might accidentally escape her. She loved Sam. Even if she refused to say so in words, the realization gripped her ferociously.

She felt apprehension creep up her spine as Sam shifted in the makeshift bed. She still knew nothing about this tall, lean man who slept beside her. He had shown her an exquisite gentleness tonight that had been delightful and surprising, but what else had he shown her of himself? Perhaps nothing about his past, but everything he did was a reflection of what was inside of him. The way he spoke, the way he carried himself, the way he touched her... all these things were Sam.

What if she took a chance, a real chance, and stayed?

# Chapter Fifteen

At daylight, Mack could wait no longer.

"Sam? Wake up."

"Mmm..." he murmured. "What is it?"

"I'm staying," she said, feeling enthusiasm rushing through her. She wondered if Sam could feel it, too.

He sat up slowly, propping himself against the railing of the tree house. His eyes were somber. She was unable to read them or his reaction. Had she risked loving him without knowing what he was willing to give in return?

"Mack, we have so much to talk about."

"What is it?" She held her breath.

"What we talked about the other night...I meant all those things about leaving. I'm not staying, Mack."

She hated that look he was giving her. She'd seen it before, twenty years earlier. And she still hated her father for it. And now she hated herself, too, for having allowed it to happen again....

THE CHOPPER LIFTED OFF, and within minutes the island was a mere speck. Then it was gone. Mack almost wondered if it had really ever existed.

She looked over at Sam. His clean-shaven appearance revealed how truly phenomenal his dark eyes were. His raven hair was slicked back into the usual queue, but he looked different. Mack questioned whether or not she would even recognize him if she met him on the street.

She closed her eyes. She had always known this fairy tale she had shared with Sam could only end with goodbye. Their make-believe world had for a brief time dissolved their disparities. When she opened her eyes, the real world loomed before them. What would Sam do now? Who would help him? She worried that he would end up on the streets again.

The ride to Virginia Beach was mercifully brief. When the chopper set down on its pad, they caught sight of the D.C. television crew that had been sent to cover their story. But Mack was through with the story. Now she simply wanted this unique experience to be over. She had failed to destroy her father's career. In fact, she had simply added one more complication to her life.

Mack was ushered off the craft first. In a matter of seconds, she was surrounded by throngs of reporters and onlookers, all straining to catch a glimpse of her and Sam. *Why?* They had called newspapers, television networks and environmental groups—all to no avail. Now Mack couldn't see two feet in front of her because of all the press people milling about.

Suddenly she became aware that Sam was out of the chopper and standing right beside her. They were trapped in the crowd together.

"Mr. McPhee," one of the reporters shouted, "Senator Anderson has publicly offered you a position with his Virginia law firm. Have you accepted?"

"What?" Mack asked.

"No comment," Sam said.

"What did he ask?" she repeated.

"Why did you quit your legal job with the city?" asked another reporter.

"McPhee! Will you be setting up a private law practice?"

Mack's eyes darted to Sam. Her legs felt hollow, weak. "Who *are* you?" she asked him.

A look of regret appeared in his eyes, and he winced as if the question had hurt him. Still, he gave no answer.

Mack stared at him as the implications of her discovery became clear in her mind. "You made a fool out of me. I want to hear you tell me why," she demanded.

"McPhee!" another reported shouted, shoving a microphone in his face. "Were you using the senator's daughter to get to him?"

Sam played catch-up in a hurry. Ignoring the reporter, he drilled Mack with his intense, dark eyes.

"The senator's *daughter?* MacKenzie Ford is MacKenzie *Anderson?*" Sam made no attempt to disguise his shock.

An awkward moment ensued as Mack merely stared at him, tongue-tied.

"Slick setup," he said. "I should compliment you on your expertise. You chopped me up and threw me to the wolves, and I never even suspected it was happening. Well done. I suppose this was your way of getting back at your father."

"Consider us even," Mack said, summoning all the hostility she could find inside herself.

*"Even?"* Sam deliberately drawled. "Why, my dear, you still have your allowance."

"McPhee!" another reporter cut in. "Please tell us what your role is here."

"Get the hell out of my way," he snarled. The crowd of reporters parted to let him pass.

Sam didn't look back, didn't slow down. He walked quickly toward a waiting car, with Mack in pursuit.

"McPhee, at least let me explain."

"You were using me to get back at your father."

"At the time, I had my reasons," she said.

Sam abruptly stopped and turned to face her. His mouth stretched slowly into a generous grin that failed to reach his narrowed eyes. "How much were you paid for selling out?"

Mack went numb. She just stood and watched as Sam entered the waiting car and sped away. This was the moment she had dreaded for so many days and nights. It was over. Just like that.

"THE FIRST RULE for a politician is that he should know how to take a stand," Sam said to the senator.

Sam had returned to D.C. Going back to what he'd left behind was the only way for him to make certain of what he really wanted.

"Do you think you're any different, Mr. Mc-Phee?" Senator Anderson asked him.

"I stated my position by coming here today and by signing over the island to you."

The office was mundane, dull, and filled to capacity with brown, aging furniture. Only the walls were alive and breathing. Pictures covered them, mostly of the senator.

"So which is it, Senator Anderson," Sam asked. "A nature reserve, or a dump site?"

"I've made my position clear."

"Convince me," Sam said. "And while you're at it, tell me what it is you want from me."

"I'll get to that in a minute." The senator buzzed an aide into his office. "Make certain this statement is delivered to the media." He paused. "Eagle Island has been donated to the College of William and Mary as a preserve to further their study of the important roles eagles and other wild birds play in the food chain. Their majestic presence inspires us all. We must all do everything possible to keep our high-flying friends soaring."

"Well done, Senator," the overly solicitous, balding aide said. "A wise choice."

The senator dismissed the matter with a wave of his hand—a prelude to turning his wrath on someone? Sam suspected that someone was him.

"So tell me, McPhee," the senator began. "Just what are your intentions concerning my daughter?"

The question hit Sam like a blow. What was it with this Anderson clan that allowed them to draw on their tempers at will? When the senator spoke again, the hard edge in his voice was gone.

"Sit down, young man. We've got some talking to do about my daughter. Tell me, do you love her?"

THE DREAM was vivid in Mack's head when she awoke. The world beyond the island was only partially real. She and Sam had been on the island for weeks—years—planning and scheming about how they would escape. . . .

Then Mack broke the illusion by getting out of her bed. Moments later, she was standing under the shower, hot water zapping clarity into her head. She thought about the tree house where she'd spent her last days with Sam, but already it was becoming less real to her. Nor could she recall the little things. In another day, she probably wouldn't even be able to recall Sam's face.

She exited the shower almost as fast as she had stepped into it. She slipped into her favorite old robe and padded into the kitchen for coffee and newspapers.

The *Washington Post* had moved as swiftly as Mack had hoped, breaking the news about the sale of the island to Senator Anderson for a dump site within days of her return to D.C. The rest of the media had then jumped on the story like a pack of wild coyotes circling a pound of red meat. The article was even carried in the senator's home state.

The editorials raised the stakes for the senator by chipping away at his credibility. Mack knew that if he went through with his plans to buy the island for a garbage dump, he would forfeit his reputation. And his reputation meant more to him than all his precious money.

Mack moved about the kitchen, shuffling over the cracked and faded linoleum, slippers flapping on the floor beneath her. The room doubled as her office. She even had a window over her desk—a sure sign of success, Mack decided. She sat at the kitchen table in her robe, a mug of tea in front of her, giving little thought to the traffic noise below.

A beep sounded from her computer, and Mack went over to investigate. Sam's credit report popped up. His accounts were maxed out, but otherwise everything looked clean. She also discovered that he had celebrated his thirty-fifth birthday on the island on August 15. And he hadn't said a word.

Business was good enough to keep Mack busy, but she had refused every call. Nothing was the same. And never would be. She was in love.

Loneliness had never entered her mind before she met Sam. Only now did she realize that her life, while it had been satisfying, had not been complete. Swell. Everyone should have a vacation on a deserted island in order to focus.

She pushed her laptop aside and spread out the *Post*. A single word jumped off the page. *Preserve.* Mack read the copy slowly. "The college cleared U.S. Senator Anderson of Virginia of any wrongdoing regarding the highly publicized dump site, and revealed that the senator had planned to turn the island into a preserve as early as five years ago. . . .''

Mack felt the blood drain from her face. Her eyes refused to focus on the print. For twenty years, Mack's life had been about revenge; now she questioned her purpose. Ironically, the time she had spent on the island trying to figure out how to destroy her father was the only time she had ever felt cared for in her life. Now nothing she did would rid her of the emptiness she had felt since leaving the island.

She stared at Sam McPhee's name on the computer screen and wondered which was worse—the crushing grief in her chest, or her deep and smoldering fury.

The intercom beeped, and Mack welcomed the diversion. ''Yes?''

''Hi.''

As Sam's voice reached her ears, a barely perceptible tremor passed through her body.

''Look out your window, Mack.''

In the street, a large and noisy crowd had gathered. The reason was the campsite Sam had set up outside her apartment complex, complete with lawn chair, umbrella and ice chest. The man was crazy! Sam was signaling for her to raise the window.

''Will you have me?'' Sam called out.

''You're nuts!''

"Yes, but I'm not homeless anymore. I'm camping out here until you say yes."

"Say yes!" came a persuasive roar from the crowd. They were definitely on Romeo's side.

"Come up and we'll talk," Mack called down, too embarrassed to continue this scene.

"I can't hear you," he said. "Come down."

"I'm in my robe."

"Do you want me to come after you?"

The man was a certifiable lunatic. Mack decided to go down to put an end to this craziness once and for all. She grabbed her keys and exited the apartment. The elevator doors parted for her. She entered and the elevator fell quickly to the lobby. She rushed past the doorman without explanation. Outside, Sam was waiting for her.

"Hi," she said, trying not to feel embarrassed about her appearance. But what did that matter? He had seen the best and the worst of her. He had saved her life. The same incredibly handsome man stood in front of her with the same incredible pull on her defenses, her self-preservation, her good intentions.

"How've you been?" he asked.

"Okay. You?"

"Okay."

"I've got news about our island."

*Our island?* Was it just a slip? Or was he hinting at some hidden meaning?

"Tell her about the job," said a familiar voice from another lawn chair.

"I'm getting to it," Sam said.

"What's my father doing here?"

"Driving us to the launch."

*"What?"*

"Give him a chance, Mack."

"Why should I?"

"Because you haven't heard his side of the story."

Overwhelmed by the sudden reappearance of both these men, Mack felt tears well up in her eyes.

"Mack, your father planned to turn the island into a preserve all along," Sam said.

"I know," she said, wiping her eyes.

"I know there's been a lot of water under the bridge," Sam began, "but there is something you should know about your father."

"Please don't do this, Sam," she barely whispered.

"Your grandmother refused to give you hundreds of his letters, Mack."

"No...I don't believe that."

"He never gave up hoping that you would look him up. She returned them to him—he still has them. He loves you, Mack."

"No..."

"Let go of the pain, Mack, all that hurt is dragging you backward. You've got *two* men who love you now. We're a package deal, your father and I."

"Why are you doing this to me?"

"Because . . . I love you."

"You love me?"

"Of course I do."

She hooked her arms around his neck and pulled his mouth to hers in a kiss that said everything.

Her future had arrived.

**Fifty red-blooded, white-hot, true-blue hunks from every State in the Union!**

Beginning in May, look for MEN MADE IN AMERICA! Written by some of our most popular authors, these stories feature fifty of the strongest, sexiest men, each from a different state in the union!

Two titles available every other month at your favorite retail outlet.

In September, look for:

DECEPTIONS by Annette Broadrick (California)
STORMWALKER by Dallas Schulze (Colorado)

In November, look for:

STRAIGHT FROM THE HEART by Barbara Delinsky (Connecticut)
AUTHOR'S CHOICE by Elizabeth August (Delaware)

**You won't be able to resist MEN MADE IN AMERICA!**

# Take 4 bestselling love stories FREE

## Plus get a FREE surprise gift!

## HARLEQUIN®

### AMERICAN ◆ ROMANCE®

Meet four of the most mysterious, magical men... when
Harlequin American Romance brings you

## MORE THAN MEN

In September, make a date to meet Alex Duporte...

*Alex* is the magic word, and he's the most wickedly
handsome genie who ever asked a woman to rub his lamp!
But what's a woman to do when a man magically dresses
her in chiffon, transforms her living room into a marbled
Mediterranean terrace, then turns himself into the sexiest
sheikh the deserts have ever seen?

Join Margaret St. George for

#### #501 A WISH...AND A KISS
September 1993

Don't miss any of the MORE THAN MEN titles.
Available wherever Harlequin books are sold.

**Where do you find hot Texas nights, smooth Texas charm and dangerously sexy cowboys?**

## *HEARTS AGAINST THE WIND*

### Strike it rich—Texas style!

Hank Travis could see himself in young Jeff Harris. The boy had oil in his blood, and wanderlust for the next big strike. There was nothing for him in Crystal Creek—except a certain marriage-minded Miss Beverly Townsend. And though Jeff seemed to have taken a shine to the former beauty queen, Hank wouldn't make book on Harris sticking around much longer!

CRYSTAL CREEK reverberates with the exciting rhythm of Texas. Each story features the rugged individuals who live and love in the Lone Star State. And each one ends with the same invitation...

### Y'ALL COME BACK...REAL SOON!
**Don't miss *HEARTS AGAINST THE WIND* by Kathy Clark
Available in September wherever Harlequin books are sold.**

# *Calloway Corners*

In September, Harlequin is proud to bring readers four
involving, romantic stories about the Calloway sisters,
set in Calloway Corners, Louisiana. Written by four of
Harlequin's most popular and award-winning authors,
you'll be enchanted by these sisters and the men
they love!

MARIAH by Sandra Canfield
JO by Tracy Hughes
TESS by Katherine Burton
EDEN by Penny Richards

As an added bonus, you can enter a sweepstakes contest
to win a trip to Calloway Corners, and meet all four
authors. Watch for details in all Calloway Corners books
in September.

CAL93

## AMERICAN ROMANCE INVITES YOU TO CELEBRATE A DECADE OF SUCCESS....

It's a year of celebration for American Romance, as we commemorate a milestone achievement—ten years of bringing you the kinds of romance novels you want to read, by the authors you've come to love.

And to help celebrate, Harlequin American Romance has a gift for you! A limited hardcover collection of two of Harlequin American Romance's most popular earlier titles, written by two of your favorite authors:

**ANNE STUART**—*Partners in Crime*
**BARBARA BRETTON**—*Playing for Time*

This unique collection will not be available in retail stores and is only available through this exclusive offer.

---

Send your name, address, zip or postal code, along with six original proof-of-purchase coupons from any Harlequin American Romance novel published in August, September or October 1993, plus $3.00 for postage and handling (check or money order—please do not send cash), payable to Harlequin Books, to:

| In the U.S. | In Canada |
|---|---|
| American Romance 10th Anniversary | American Romance 10th Anniversary |
| Harlequin Books | Harlequin Books |
| P.O. Box 9057 | P.O. Box 622 |
| Buffalo, NY 14269-9057 | Fort Erie, Ontario |
| | L2A 5X3 |

(Please allow 4-6 weeks for delivery. Hurry! Quantities are limited. Offer expires November 30, 1993.)

---

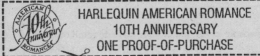

HARLEQUIN AMERICAN ROMANCE
10TH ANNIVERSARY
ONE PROOF-OF-PURCHASE                092-KBA